1st SIGNED

D0397826

FIELD NOTES

For Raman —

with a sense of
pleasure at our
collaboration —

Barry Lopez

Also by Barry Lopez

FIELD NOTES

The Grace Note of the Canyon Wren

BARRY LOPEZ

 Alfred A. Knopf   New York   1994

THIS IS A BORZOI BOOK
PUBLISHED BY ALFRED A. KNOPF, INC.

Some of the stories from this work were originally published
in the following publications: *North American
Review* ("The Entreaty of the Wiideema"), *Orion* ("Lessons from
the Wolverine"), and *Outside* magazine ("Pearyland").

Library of Congress Cataloging-in-Publication Data
Lopez, Barry Holstun, [date]
Field notes : the grace note of the canyon wren / by
Barry Lopez—1st ed.
p.   cm.
ISBN 0-679-43453-4
I. Title.
PS3562.O67F54   1994
813'.54—dc20   94-2144   CIP

Manufactured in the United States of America
First Edition

For

James F. Andrews (1936–1980)

for

A. Gunn, P. Morel, B. Taylor, and E. Tracy

and

Sue Hertel (1931–1993)

CONTENTS

FIELD NOTES

INTRODUCTION: WITHIN BIRDS' HEARING

I am enfeebled by this torrent of light. Each afternoon seems the last for me. Hammered by the sun, mapless in country but vaguely known, I am like a desiccated pit lying in a sand wash. Hope has become a bird's feather, glissading from the evening sky.

The journey started well enough. I left my home in the eastern Mojave twelve or fifteen days ago, making a path for the ocean. Like a sleek cougar I crossed the Lloma Hills, then the Little Sangre de

Cristo Range. I climbed up out of the southernmost extension of White Shell Canyon without incident. Early on, the searing heat made me wary, brought me to consider traveling only at night. But, the night skies cast with haze and so near a new moon, it was impossible to find my way.

Today I thought it might rain. But it does not seem likely now. It's been more difficult to locate water than I've known in the past, and that lack in this light and heat has added to my anxiety. Also, my grasp of how far I still have to travel is imperfect. This most of all fills me with dread.

In the distance, the stony, cactus-strewn land falls down into the drainage of the Curandera. I will turn north here this morning and hope to be in the wet canyon of the Oso by nightfall and down off this high blistered plain. From there, however far it may be, I know the river will flow to the ocean. It's comforting, each evening, to construe the ocean as my real destiny—the smooth beach underfoot, round and hard like an athlete's thigh, the ocean crashing, shaking off the wind, surging up the beach slope, all of it like wild horses. But, walking the Oso, I could come upon some sign that might direct me elsewhere, perhaps north into the Rose Peaks, into country I do not know at all.

Part of the difficulty of this journey has been having to feel my way like this. I departed—my body deft, taut—with a clear image of where I should go: the route, the dangers, the distances by day. But then the landscape became vast. Thinking too much on the end, I sometimes kept a pace poorly matched to the country. By evening I was winded, irritated, dry hearted. I would scrape out a place on the ground and fall asleep, too exhausted to eat. My clothing, thin and worn, began to disintegrate. I would awaken dreamless, my tongue swollen from thirst, and look about delirious for any companion—a dog, a horse, another human being just waking up. But there was no one with whom to speak, no one even to offer water to. I spat my frustration out. I pushed on, resolute as Jupiter's moons, breaking down only once, weeping and licking the earth.

I did not anticipate the ways in which I would wear out.

My one salvation, a gift I can't reason through, has been the unceasing kindness of animals. Once, when I was truly lost, when the Grey Spider Hills and the Black Sparrow Hills were entirely confused in a labyrinth of memory, I saw a small coyote sitting between two creosote bushes just a few yards away. She was eyeing me quizzically, whistling me up with that look. I followed behind her without question, into country that eventually made sense to me, or which I eventually remembered.

Another time, the eighth day out, I fainted, collapsing from heat and thirst onto the cobble plain through the blood shimmer of air. I was as overwhelmed by my own foolishness, as struck down by the arrogance in my determination as I was overcome by thirst. Falling, I knew the depth of my stupidity, but not as any humiliation. I felt unshackled. Released. I came back to the surface aware of drops of water trickling into my throat. I tried to raise an arm to the harrowing sun but couldn't lift the weight. I inhaled the texture of warm silk and heard a scraping like stiffened fans. When I squinted through quivering lashes I saw I was beneath birds.

Mourning doves were perched on my chest, my head, all down my legs, their wings flared above me like parasols. They held my lips apart with slender toes. One by one, doves settled on my cheeks. They craned their necks at angles to drip water, then flew off. Their gleaming eyes were an infant's lucid pools.

Backed into this rock shelter, out of the sun's first, slanting rays, I am trying to manufacture now a desire to go on, to step once again into a light I must stroke through. The light wears like acid and the heat to come will terrorize even lizards. It is not the desert of my childhood.

I concentrate on an image of transparent water and cool air flowing through the Oso River Canyon, beyond the horizon. I will lie down naked in its current. Cool watercress will stick like rose petals to my skin. I will anoint my eyes, my fevered ears. I will lap water like a shaking dog. The fired plain before me, the wicked piercing of thorns, my knotted intestines, the lost path I will endure for that. Drawing the two together in my mind—the eviscerating heat, the forgiving water—I see the horizons of my life. My desire to arrive, to cover this distance, is so acute I whimper like a colt when I breathe.

Two days past, in Agredecido Canyon, I came upon a gallery of wild figures painted on a sheer rock escarpment a thousand years ago. I was walking on the far side of the wash and nearly missed them, concealed behind a row of tall cottonwoods. So many days in a landscape without people had made me anxious and I went quickly across, as though they were alive and could speak.

Someone's ancestors had drawn thirty-four figures on the sienna rock, many familiar and comforting—mountain sheep running, human figures traveling, and other animals free of gravity, as if they were plummeting toward the sky. Huge kachinalike demigods were dancing. A square-shouldered human form stood with its back turned, holding a snake. Two perplexing images attracted me. One was a series of pictographs, lined out along a cleft in the rock. The initial drawing, the one farthest to the left as I read them, was of a single bush, like sagebrush. Then came a clump of thin, thready lines, lightly incised. Then a rope coil with tattered ends and then a second rope, unwound and undulating. Lastly, a cast of double curves, like a child's sea gulls flying away.

The second image was simpler, a bear tumbling on the spout of a shooting geyser. I thought it a water geyser, but the bear's large eyes and the round shape of its mouth revealed such fear that finally I believed it a geyser of blood. As with so much of what people leave behind, it's difficult to say what was meant. We can only surmise that they loved, that they were afraid.

I rise and press off. From beneath a paloverde I take a bearing on the high white disk of the sun. Looking toward the indistinct middle distance, the outwash plain of distorted mountains, I believe I am looking at the shoulder of the place where the waters of the Oso will rise.

I stride along this route just north of west, listening

to the seething cut of the sickle light, feeling the black heat rise around me like water, watchful where I step. My eye is out sharply for any track, for the camouflage in which poisonous snakes hide. I find a good pace and work to hold it, adjusting breath and stride as I cross arroyos with their evidence of flash floods and climb and descend shallow hills. I do not think of the Oso at all but only of what is around me—the powdery orange of globe mallow blossoms, lac glistening on wands of creosote bushes, bumble-bees whining. The afternoon, the prostrate sky, sweep on. My feet crumble the rain pan and wind pack of dust. Breezes whisk scorched seeds toward me. The seeds, bits of brittle leaf and stem, corral my feet and lie still.

At one point I see antelope—so far south for these animals, twenty or more of them ranging to the south-east, an elongation of life under the heaved sky.

At last light, when the sun has set beneath the mountains, I am without a trace of the Oso. I sit down on a granite boulder, a slow collapse onto the bone of my haunches. The country has clearly proved more than I can imagine. I consider that I began this morning confidently, rightly seasoned I believed, and then, with every conscious fiber, I feel I will not despair. My body comes back erect with determina-tion. I have made so many miles today. But I know—

I have no good day past this one. Desperation, the heavy night tide, surges. I cannot stand again. My feet throb from stone bruises and thorn punctures. My flesh spills the shrieking heat. My tongue wads my mouth. I bow my head, my sticking eyelids, to my knees. Into this agony, as if from an unsuspected room, comes a bare cascade of sound. My wounds become silent. The long phrase descends again, a liquid tremolo. The skin over my cheekbones chills, as when sweat suddenly dries. Again the falling *ti-yew*, *tiyew*, *tiyew*, *tiyew*, and, a turn at the end, *tew*.

I stand up to rivet the dimness. The burbling call breaks the dark once more. This time I hear each note, a canyon wren, surely, but something else. I strain my ears at the night, listening for that other sound. When it comes I realize it has been there each time, each call, an ornament hardly separated from the bird's first note. I recall vividly the last canyon wrens I heard, ones around my home where they are never far from the waters of the Colorado, their voices another purling in the dry air.

The song again, pure, sharp, now without the grace note. I fix its place and move into the night, my face averted, feeling through the darkness with my hands, sliding my feet ahead, down a scrabble slope. Long minutes pass between bursts of wren song and then there is only silence. I am standing in water for some moments before I am aware of its caress, before I can separate the pain in my feet from its soothing. A little farther on I hear the gurgle of springs. More water, running from beneath the Sierra de San Martín. I squat down to feel the expanse of the shallow flow. Headwaters of the Oso.

I walk a little ways, down the gathering waters.

I drink. I bathe. I rinse out my clothes.

The ocean is far away, but I feel its breath booming against the edge of the continent. Wind evaporating water tightens my bare flesh. I feel the running tide of my own salted blood. In the full round air from below I can detect, though barely, a perfume of pear blossoms and wetted fields. I can distinguish in it the last halt cries of birds, becalmed in the marshes.

TEAL
CREEK

I n the Magdalena Mountains east of Ordell, in country that's been called the Bennett River country since the time of white people, an anchorite (as I would later come to understand the word) settled. His name was James Teal. He drove in when trillium were in full flower, April of 1954, in a green 1946 Dodge and stayed first for several weeks at the Courtyard Motel in Ordell before moving up onto the Bennett.

He brought no remarkable possessions. He

walked with a slight limp, which my father thought might be from a war wound. He was tall, lean, his face vaguely Asiatic. I remember people noticed right away that he was not an intruder, and was easy to speak to. For a stranger who didn't have a job, or a way of life that fit him anywhere, he drew remarkably little suspicion in Ordell. Days, he was out of town in his car—people saw him walking in and out of the woods at different places; evenings he spent around the motel. He ate supper at Dan and Ruella's cafe or the Vincent Hotel. He didn't go into the bars. He bought groceries, like everyone, at Clyde's on Assiniboine—that's long gone now—and bought rope and pipe and things at Cassidy's Feed, which had a hardware section back then.

People like my father who always watched everything just a little said they saw less of him as summer went on. I don't remember, really, seeing much of him myself. I was infatuated with Esther Matthews and I missed a lot then, I suppose. But by the end of summer, August, he was gone.

After that, from the winter of '54–'55 on, he lived up on the Bennett. He gave the Dodge over to Wilton Haskin, who owned the Courtyard—some say he traded the car for rent or tools or meals, but if he did it was Wilton who likely got the better end of the deal. Wilton drove the car until he died in the fall of 1975. Then his son Clarence drove it another ten years.

Teal lived in two places I knew of on tributaries off the Bennett. One was at Cougar Creek and the other was on Lesley Creek, though for some reason then we called it White Dog Creek and now, like myself, some people call it Teal Creek.

Teal understood very well how to get on alone up there. He found spots where hot springs surfaced near south-facing benches, where he had light enough for a garden—which meant he looked the country over more closely than anyone I ever knew, or heard of. I was only inside the second cabin he built, but the first one must have been much like it, tight and simple. He broke and moved a lot of rock at the second place, a terrible amount of work, really, to make a good foundation for a one-room cabin. And he built a flume there at the second place, a wood chute to carry the flow of water from the hot spring through at floor level. He packed a woodstove in and had creek water, and he built a porch big enough to cover some of his firewood and a daybed.

I was thirteen the summer he moved up on Cougar Creek. I didn't go up that way to hunt or wander or fool around. No one did. At the time all the country around there was so open, so empty of people, no one much kept him in mind. He wasn't any trespasser. It was all federal land. We would see him in town once or twice, early in the spring or late in summer. He'd work a few weeks for Wilton, buy staples at Clyde's, and then hitch back out to Bennett River. From the highway he'd walk up Cougar Creek to his place or, later, the four miles up White Dog Creek.

Those times he'd hitch back out of town, once I got my license, I'd think about offering him a ride. He was the most beguiling person to me, beckoning, like the first pungent smell of cottonwood buds. He seemed as independent and benign as the moon. But I was shy and my father disapproved of that kind of curiosity.

I went away to college in '59. Summers I worked with my father, a heavy-equipment contractor. In the summer after my junior year we were building logging roads back up from the Bennett. One night, halfway home, I missed my wallet and turned the truck around, certain it had fallen out at the work site. I found it on the ground alongside the grader I was driving. By then it was after seven, but the sky was still bright, and I got to thinking about James Teal. Without knowing why, without really looking at what I was doing, I pulled off the road at Lesley Creek bridge and sat there. I wanted to see his place. I wanted to talk with him. Where did he come from? What sort of things did he work at? Did he have a family somewhere? I wondered if he was purely white, but I wouldn't admit to the rank curiosity, the willingness to invade his privacy. I'd never had a conversation with the man. I had no reason at all to be calling.

Still, that evening I went up the creek. Dusk was long enough to see by for a few hours and I carried a flashlight to come back. I walked along a deer trail, just a few yards into the trees, a narrow path cushioned with moss and fir needles. No stranger would guess a man occasionally passed there.

It was dark when I finally descried the cabin. I saw its angles silhouetted in trees against the sky. Teal was standing on the porch, looking into the woods, but not toward me. In hearth or candle light I saw he wore a white T-shirt tucked in his trousers and that he was barefoot. I squatted down on the trail. Two Swainson's thrushes were calling, back and forth. After a while they were quiet and Teal went in. I heard the door close, the metal latch fall.

I felt foolish and at the same time a little frightened. I'd come all this way, then said nothing, and had hidden from the man. I couldn't understand why I was scared, but I got so dizzy I had to sit. I felt myself in a kind of sinkhole in the darkness. I knew if I walked up to the cabin and spoke to him I'd be all right. But I turned back on the deer trail. My skin prickled. I ran fast, imagining feral dogs chasing me down. I tangled in limbs and blackberry vines. All the way out to the road I felt an edge of panic.

At the truck I calmed myself. It wasn't Teal that had frightened me. It wasn't the dark, either. What scared me was the thought that I might have injured him. I knew right then what it meant to trespass.

Late in the summer of 1967, I moved back to Ordell and went to work full-time for my father. I had married a woman named Julie Quiros from Stuart River. I'd finished four years in the army, none of it, I've always been grateful, in Vietnam, and we'd had a daughter, Blair. My mother's younger brother, despondent, involved with another woman, had shot himself and his wife, and their three children, all girls, had come to live with my parents. Clyde Brennan had closed his store and another market had opened up.

Teal, like the first wildly colored harlequin duck I ever saw, had been somewhere at the edge of my thoughts all that time, ever since that night. When I got home I asked my father if he'd seen him recently. He said yes, Teal had been in town that August, had worked a little for Wilton, the same as always, then he'd gone back out to his place—and certainly, whether it was federal land or not, it *was* his place by now.

What could he believe in? I wondered. What allowed him to be comfortable out there from one year to the next? Whatever his beliefs were, he didn't bother anybody with them. Whenever he came to town he got on easily with people. I remember even a few times he played softball with us, laughing as much as anyone when he dropped easy pop flies or struck out. Did he keep a tidy shelf of books up there? And which books would those be? Did he reel and crouch in the moon's light?

Though I'd never done so as a boy, I knew there were spots along the Bennett good to swim in, and on an Indian summer day in September of '67 I took Julie and Blair up to a place past Teal Creek. They swam. I couldn't keep my attention on them. I felt my unseemly curiosity, the cowardice and insistence of it, and I knew Julie was aware that something was running in my mind.

I looked over at her, at the soft, veined line of her neck, where it rose from her shoulders.

"You know that fellow Teal?" I asked.

"The hermit?"

"I don't know, really." After a while I said, "When I was fourteen, a man named Ephraim Lincoln told all of us a story about Teal, one morning at Clyde's during hunting season. He said he found where Teal had walked barefoot in the snow and seen where he'd knelt down for a long time by a little waterfall, then lay out full, naked. I shook my head and laughed right along with the older men, but everyone knew that the scorn was wrong, misdirected. It was Ephraim who was lewd, a corrupt individual.

"Ever since then, I've known I wanted to protect Teal. And that I should—that I'm meant to—receive something from him. I don't know what it is."

Julie rested her fingers on my arm.

That fall instead of going up Enid River to look for deer with a friend I went alone up the Bennett. I planned to walk in along Cougar Creek and just roam around. If I saw Teal's first cabin, well, fine. I'd look it over. I knew I wouldn't shoot any deer up there, no matter. It would have been wrong, mixing those things.

I got about a mile up Cougar Creek and then knew I shouldn't be in there. I turned back, feeling a familiar dread and misgiving. Then, a short way down the trail, I was fine. It occurred to me that maybe Teal was dealing with menace, that out here he went chin to chin with an evil I could not imagine. The knowledge that he might do this shamed me. Where was my own courage, my own resolution?

That winter I began reading to Blair at night. We started off with fairy tales, but the most interesting stories to us after a while were Indian stories, ones

collected by George Bird Grinnell and James Willard
Schultz from Cheyenne and Blackfeet and Gros Ven-
tre people not so far away, over in Montana and
Wyoming. At first I thought Blair would be bored.
The stories were mostly about young men traveling,
or about the creation of the world. But she liked
them. The stories were simple, without irony. They
had a disarming morality to them that I enjoyed
experiencing with her. When a story ended, Julie
would hug us together and say, "And that's how the
world really is. It's a true story." Later, when they'd
gone to bed, I'd sit with some of the books and
wonder about the Creation, and what it was, really,
that kept the world from flying apart.

The year after I returned to Ordell my father had
a heart attack and asked me to take over the business. Our lawyer drew up the papers and it was all
done in a few days. My father had fifteen men working for him. I wasn't eager for the responsibility.

The following spring I decided to go visit Teal.
One morning I just got in the truck and drove up the
Bennett. If he asked me why I'd come I was going
to say I didn't know. I felt bound to, I'd say. I wasn't
going to make something up.

It was raining when I left the house and pouring
by the time I got to Teal Creek. I followed the deer
trail all the way in to the cabin. From a clearing in

front of the porch, another trail went between trees over a rise and out onto a treeless bench. I saw Teal standing out there in the downpour, beyond the green rows of a new garden. He was bent far over before the flat gray sky in what appeared to be an attitude of prayer or adoration, his arms at his sides. The rain had plastered his shirt to his back and his short black hair glistened. He did not move at all while I stood there, fifteen or twenty minutes. And in that time I saw what it was I had wanted to see all those years in James Teal. The complete stillness, a silence such as I had never heard out of another living thing, an unbroken grace. He was wound up in the world, neat and firm as a camas bulb in the ground, and spread out over it like three days of weather. The wind beat down on James Teal. Beyond him clouds snagged in the fir trees. The short growth in his garden between us was fresh and bright. When I turned to leave, the cabin looked lean, compact as a hunting heron.

That night when I lay with Julie I described the scene and told her the details, the history of my long desire to know James Teal, a desire that seemed, in that moment, to have abated. Two years later, on a balmy Saturday afternoon in May 1971, I again felt compelled to visit him, as though he had called to me from a dream. I found him slumped in a chair at an outside table, the remains of his lunch before him. Sparrows flew up from crumbs on the white porcelain plate. He had been dead only a few hours, I guessed.

I moved him over to the porch floor, laid him out there with his arms over his chest, and went inside to look for a blanket. I never before saw a room so obviously lived in, so hand and foot worn, so spare as that one. Beside the bed was a table and stool. The iron stove, a storage box, a single shelf with pans and dishes and some books. At one of the two windows was a sort of kneeler, which I later learned was called a prie-dieu.

I covered James Teal's body with a yellow blanket from his cot and walked out to the road. I sat there in the truck with the door propped open for a long time, reluctant to start the tasks that would bring the sheriff and the coroner and perhaps others up Teal Creek. We were reading a story just then, Julie and Blair and I, about how First Person was going to create bright, metallic dragonflies, cutthroat trout, short-eared owls, elk, and the other animals. I had not looked ahead as sometimes I do, but I imagined reading that evening about animals filling up the world. I imagined it would make us feel fine and grateful. Reading it aloud would make us feel as if nothing would go wrong.

EMPIRA'S

TAPESTRY

*T*he fall Empira Larson came to Idora we remember not solely for her arrival but for the height of the drought. Winter rains the year before never filled the creeks. The following summer the woods were parched and brittle and we worried terribly about fire, though none came. It wasn't until Christmas that the creeks came up and the river filled.

Empira came to teach fourth grade. She boarded with me her first six months, then moved to a small house that needed repairs and was always damp, but which gave her a depth of privacy people like her seem to crave. It was my own feeling that she had arrived on the heels of some difficulty with a man—not necessarily something he had caused, either; but I didn't inquire and wouldn't have. She showed a sharp tongue if provoked but otherwise had a fine bearing and was gracious with the children. She seemed to live the life before her, not one left behind.

To be truthful, I wasn't much drawn to her at first nor did I welcome her friendship. After my husband died I felt an odd antagonism toward younger women, especially women like Empira who had made independent lives for themselves, who moved about the country freely and might have had many lovers. Empira's presence made me look poorly on my own life. In conversations with her, meal after meal, I came to know an anger that had not touched me before.

During the weeks she stayed with me I tried to regard Empira as irresponsible and self-important; but nothing in her could long sustain such a view. I held it from self-pity, I later realized. Or envy. When she moved out I missed her company so much it unnerved me. She had dispelled an atmosphere of complacency in my house, as no other boarder ever had. She was fresh as flowers. A boy staying with me briefly began to swagger around the house in such a way you could see he assumed Empira was just smitten. One night he asked her in a smug, condescending way to go to the movies. She said, "Mr. Conway, I love going to the movies, but I'm afraid I wouldn't enjoy them very much with you." She could be that blunt, but Eldon Beemis was the single one of my long-term boarders glad to see her go. It gave him the table back, to run the supper conversation as he wished.

A year after she moved out, Empira and I and Albert Garreau, who owned the mercantile, and Deborah Purchase, another widow, were sitting in the school cafeteria after a trip with the students. We'd been out to the Pearson Prehistoric Shelter, a cave above the river east of town. It was warm. We'd gotten cool drinks. With end-of-the-day weariness we were musing about how long ago the shelter had been occupied by humans—eight thousand years, too far back for us to imagine. Albert began recounting the history of Idora, which of course seemed ephemeral by comparison. I recalled a story of my grandfather's time—he'd come to Idora in 1871 with the railroad—and that one led to another.

My grandfather's stories of Ohio and the Great Plains, and of his many trips to the Pacific and the Gulf, were ones I'd committed to memory. The language I used when I told them was different from my own. It had my grandfather's precision and force.

I got caught up in his stories that day. I talked until the cafeteria was so dark I couldn't see the others' faces clearly. Albert, whom I found appealing partly because he listened to everyone so attentively, had heard many of the stories before, one following on another like a stream of water. Deborah had too. Empira's attention was rapt.

When I stopped talking I felt slightly chagrined, having gone on so long with such enthusiasm. But telling the stories always had that effect on me. I felt them physically, even—Grandfather's descriptions of wind-tossed oceans of grass in Nebraska, of huge trees in the valley bottoms of western Oregon, of flocks of cranes flying over. People's desires: ". . . when Adrian tasted the wheat flour, the faint trace of nasturtiums was there. He bought every bag Edward Bonner had on the shelves." When I spoke of these things, it was as if I were guiding a canoe through rapids and stretches of calm water, conveying my passengers on a momentous journey down a marked but unknown path. I rose to this part of my life as I did to no other.

When Albert and then Deborah left, Empira invited me to her home for supper. I said I wasn't able to come. I wouldn't like eating in that small, dank, ramshackle house of hers. I was ashamed of myself, thinking so; and when she told me then how won-

drous and strange and invigorating my stories were
I felt worse. She said they were an homage to my
grandfather's memory; she said that I was their custo-
dian, and that when I told the stories I was beautiful.

My eyes filled with tears right in front of her. I
couldn't help it.

Empira was a physically active woman and early on
volunteered to coach girls' track at the high school,
though I don't believe she knew much about it at the
beginning. One Saturday morning when I was leaving
for Blue River, I saw her on the cinder track behind
the school and pulled over to watch her from the car.
Lap after lap she ran, her cheeks red, her head
bobbing, her stride too short to be graceful but re-
lentless. I was mesmerized by her belief in herself,
at the same time I questioned it.

You couldn't say what Empira cared about most.
She was a good teacher, by all that I heard. Her
concern for the children was genuine and tireless.
She read voraciously and had a lot of music she
listened to. She didn't visit much, but she carried
the irksome burden of a single woman in Idora with
no self-consciousness I saw. Several town men,
aimless strays, foisted themselves on her. When
she didn't give them what they wanted they moved
on. I wondered if Empira cared at all about having

a man in her life. I suspected she did, and it irritated me that she pretended it didn't. Men new to town would hear around that she was "an eccentric, selfish bitch"—that's what Albert Garreau told me when I asked. It took me a while to understand what they resented was her insistence on privacy and independence.

The third year Empira was among us she discovered she was sick. She never spoke of it directly, but I remember she came by the house one day with a book for me—we often traded mysteries—and she gave me an ebony stick at the same time. She said it was a storyteller's stick, from Ghana. The storyteller drew in the dirt with it, she said, while he spoke. I think of that as the moment she told me she was dying.

In that last year—a long summer, then the rainiest winter I can remember, a late spring—Empira began a tapestry. I'd gotten over my feelings about her house, knowing by then what lay behind them, and when I went over for supper one night I saw the loom set up on the side porch. On it was the most astonishing piece of handwork I had ever seen. An understanding swept over me then that Empira was gifted in a way I could barely comprehend. Despite her usually good manners, Empira would deliberately annoy people on occasion if she felt they were being self-righteous—and she could be aloof. In my pettiness, I must say I enjoyed the few small barbs and comeuppances she suffered because of this. I thought they showed her her limits. But when I stood in front of that tapestry my stomach dropped. I never felt the same about her again.

When I first looked at it I thought it had to be a painting, so fine was her weave. Only with my glasses on could I distinguish the threads one from another or, more amazing, the boundaries between colors. A hundred spools of thread pegged on a board ran the spectrum from plum through saffron to ruby red, with dozens of shades of blue and green and hues of brown.

The tapestry was but a quarter finished, only the left margin and most of the upper left corner done. It would be about five feet by three, a wilderness scene of bright sunlight over a canyon. A few words had been sewn in over the shadows of trees in the left foreground.

"Empira," I whispered, raising my hands in astonishment, in a kind of helplessness.

"When I was a little girl," she told me, "my parents took my brothers and me to the Grand Canyon. You can actually see all that space over the canyon, you know. I never forgot its breadth, how delicate the colors of the rocks and the sky and the trees were that hung in it. I wanted to fill that space up, to be inside it like a bird, graceful, rising, falling, flying long, winding spirals from the rim down to a landing far below."

"What are the words, here, what are they going to be?"

"What I wrote the first morning after I was married. They are my sentences of greatest desire, the purest hope I think I ever wrote."

I waited for her to go on.

"I don't regret the feelings, not a word," she said, chiding me for my presumption.

"Empira, if you can weave this well, I mean with such skill, which is really so completely—"

"It's each individual thread, Marlis. Tying off each single thread. Pulling them from the spools, holding them to the light, feeling their tension, like violin strings, before they become part of the pattern."

"But it's so beautiful. And, my God, so real. You've hidden your lamp under a bushel basket."

"We suspect so little of what goes on in the world, of what is happening or has happened to us. We don't gather the threads, Marlis. We let them go and then the wind weaves them. We let go and float. We eddy up along the river somewhere, most of us, and just wait out our time."

By early that summer, when classes were over, we could see Empira was exhausted and we knew that she was ill. But none of us, the circle of her friends—Albert, Deborah, Ellie Randall, who was the principal, Dick Everson, who taught with her, or Grady and Maureen Sillings, who lived next door to me—none of us felt it right to bring it up. She had a pattern to her life that was deliberate and private, and this was but the last part of it.

That summer she visited each child she'd taught—of those that still lived nearby—giving some of them books and trinkets. When fall came she wasn't strong enough to teach and Ellie told her not to come in. Empira visited me regularly, sometimes bringing flowers. She encouraged and then listened with such pleasure to my stories. She aged in those weeks, physically, but her temperament became more serene, and as I listened to her speak of her own past I heard no self-pity or recrimination. I knew then that I loved her.

She finished the tapestry but didn't tell me. I saw it at her house one morning, still on the loom. The completed scene was brilliant, almost luminous. The air filling the canyon was bright and depthless but it had the pale color she'd described. The words were unobtrusive. As I bent down to read them I was struck with an enormous sadness. "My holy and blooded desire . . . implausible as such a life can be . . . his hands tracing the bow of my back, his lips on the rim of my ear . . . bring my own children here, to find what I was given . . ."

It rained without letup that October, not the mist and unending drizzle we are used to but downpours that flooded the air and streamed over the ground, night and day. One evening, Empira came to my door and said when I opened it, "Will you walk with me this evening, Mrs. Damien?"

I said yes, of course. We walked through the rain, down streets that led from homes on the hills to stores that fronted the highway and the park, then the river. Her stride was short, her steps firm. She spoke as we went, as her strength allowed.

"You have a good memory, Marlis," she began. "Perhaps you will do me the favor of remembering all I will try to say now." I feared she would become philosophical, but she was specific, enumerating things in her house, saying to whom each was to go. A set of tattered place mats, a raw amethyst in its mother stone, a Steuben vase, a box of hummingbird

feathers. Some of her choices, the beneficiaries, surprised me.

We crossed the highway and walked through the
park. The muddy river, visible in the faint glow of
street lamps, undulated powerfully. Empira guided
us to a place where it rose to the very edge of the
bank. I understood her intention in the same moment
that she made a gesture with her hand to sever us. I
acquiesced, against all my beliefs. She dropped her
coat to the ground, pulled a shawl more tightly
around her, stepped out of her shoes and moved to
the river's edge. After a moment she sank down and
lay over on her side. I couldn't tell then whether she
moved or whether the river surged but the water rose
under her and enveloped her and she was gone. Her
dress crumpled last in the grip of the current and I
saw that the shawl was her tapestry turned side to.

She was gone quickly, as if it hadn't happened,
as if I were still listening to her voice on the hilly
streets.

Two days later her body surfaced miles away in a
flood eddy. I found an address for her family, a small
town in eastern Pennsylvania. Her mother said there
was no reason to send her back, not all that way at
such expense. Could we please bury her there? she
asked. We did, at the best spot Ellie and Albert and

I could find at the Idora cemetery. The Reverend Arthur Thorven read an impatient service, annoyed by what he believed was a sinful act of despair, a failure of courage. It was a first funeral for most of the children. They looked on in awe, troubled, disbelieving. Some people standing there may have thought what Eldon Beemis had at breakfast that morning, opening the paper as I cleared the dishes.

"Says here Empira had cancer. Homeliness, I expect, was the root of what got her. Why she killed herself."

I felt so sharply in that moment the poverty of my friendship.

THE

OPEN

LOT

*J*ane Weddell took any of several routes from her apartment on West Sixty-fourth Street to the museum on West Seventy-seventh, depending. Her path was determined by a pattern of complexity outside her thought, the result not solely of her emotional state but also of her unconscious desire, say, to avoid a wind blowing black grit down Columbus Avenue on the morning when she was wearing a new blouse for the first time. Or she gave in to whim, following a path defined by successive flights of pigeons, a path that might lead her east down Seventy-third Street to the park instead of across on Seventy-fifth or Sixty-eighth.

The pattern of her traverses from one day to the next gave her a sense of the vastness in which she lived; she was aware not only of the surface of each street but, simultaneously, of the tunneling below, which carried water mains and tree roots, like the meandering chambers of gophers. And ranging above, she knew without having to look, were tiers upon tiers of human life, the joy and anger and curiosity of creatures like herself.

She arrived by one or another of her footpaths—she imagined them, lying awake at night, like a *rete mirabile*, a tracery over the concrete, the tar, and the stone—at a room on the second floor of the Museum of Natural History, a vaulted, well-lit space in which she worked six or seven hours a day, preparing fossils of marine organisms from the Cambrian period and the Precambrian era. It was her gift to discern in the bits of rock placed before her lines of such subtlety that no one who beheld her excisions could quite believe what she had done. Under the bold, piercing glass of a microscope, working first with the right hand and then, when the muscles in that hand lost their strength, the left, she removed clay and sand and silt, grain by grain, her eyes focused on suggestions indescribably ambivalent. When she finished and set the piece apart, one saw in stone a creature so complete, even to the airiness of its antennae, that it rivaled something living.

From an inchoate maze of creatures alive in the early Paleozoic, she released animal after animal, turned them loose for others to brood over. And from these creatures the systematists cantilevered names, a precarious litany; it was hard to believe that among things so trenchant, despite their silence, names so bloodless would adhere. What was certain was that from a piece of stone in which a creature *might* reside—guessing simply from the way light broke on its surface—Jane Weddell would pry an animal wild as a swamp night.

The shadow across Jane Weddell's life did not come from living alone, a condition that offered her a peace she esteemed like fresh water; nor from being patronized for her great gift by people who avoided her company. It was thrown by the geometry of a life her professional colleagues implied was finally innocuous. No one, perhaps no one in the world, could make the essential pieces of the first puzzle of Earthly life so apparent. But in the eyes of her associates she wandered thoughtlessly outside any orthodoxy in discussing fossils. She strayed from recognized subdivisions of geological time, so people had trouble agreeing on the value of her ideas. Many tried to give meaning to what she did; but because she would neither insist upon nor defend any one theoretical basis for her thought she was ultimately regarded as a technician only. The pattern in her work, what propelled her to the next thing and then the next, was the joy of revelation. She saw no greater purpose in life than to reveal and behold.

What Jane Weddell rendered was conveyed solemnly from the room in which she worked by people who behaved as though they bore off brittle sheaves of IV dynasty papyrus. In adjoining rooms, each creature was photographed, matched to a technical description she provided, inventoried, and given space in a protective case. Frequently, her exacting descriptions were marked for the attention of one of several researchers who, from this alien menagerie, sought to fathom an ecology of early sea floors. Jane Weddell's memory for any particular fossil was thorough and unconfused; and she understood how the details in this complex, ramulose array of images were related through extraordinary subtleties of shape—but she was rarely consulted. Systematists might ponder at their computer screens for weeks looking for ecological relationships Jane Weddell could have articulated in a moment, if anyone had conveyed to her how they anticipated fitting every-thing—even these most rarefied forms of early life—together.

She listened politely to urgings that she concen-trate on figuring out taxonomic sequences, or that she stick, say, to the Middle Silurian for a while; but she didn't follow through. She hoped, instead, someone might ask what the difference was between two trilobites of the same species where one had been extricated from its matrix with the music of Bach in her ears, the other with Haydn. She wanted to say that there were differences; for her, the preci-sion the systematists sought in their genealogies, even with a foundation as exquisite as the one she provided, was a phantom, a seduction.

In an empty lot on West Seventy-fifth—one that had been cleared of its building and then abandoned to grow up in weeds, feral grasses, and ailanthus trees—Jane Weddell occasionally saw phantoms. It was a peripheral sensation, not anything viewed di-rectly but only glimpsed, like a single bird, high up, disappearing between two buildings. The existence of the lot exerted a pressure upon her, like a wind growing imperceptibly but steadily more forceful.

The lot was separated from the sidewalk by a

gateless, chain-link fence and shadowed east and west by windowless walls of brick. To the north it was closed off by a high, gray-board fence. One ailanthus, in the far western corner, shaded several hundred square feet. In spring, the grasses grew waist high and among the tall and running weeds purple aster, small white daisy fleabane, and yellow coltsfoot bloomed. In winter the lot fell comatose, exposing a soil of crushed brick and cement powder where shards of glass glinted beside matchbook covers and aluminum cans and where rainwater beaded up on cigarette packs.

Jane Weddell found the lot alluring. One evening when she was walking back late from the museum she saw a small creature run out through the fence and beneath a parked car. She watched motionless for many minutes; then movement on the lip of a trash barrel halfway down the block drew her eye. It was the same animal, discarding some odd bit of debris and falling back into shadow again.

It disturbed Jane Weddell's sense of grace and proportion to be drawn any more to one place than another; she resisted the desire to pass by the lot more frequently once it began to occupy her waking mind. But her sense of perception now grew more acute as she drew near, prepared to catch the faintest signal; and her peripheral awareness intensified. She took in the sky, the shudder of the street beneath her feet, the roll and ruffle of the stout limbs of a London plane tree nearby. To perceive the lot clearly, she believed, she must gain a sense of the whole pattern of which it was a part, taking in even passing cars, the smell of garbage cans, the shriek of schoolchildren.

The lot slowly changed. Through the weeks of spring, and while summer grasses rose up vigorously, bits of broken pipe, a length of coaxial cable, coffee containers, pills of gum foil, a strip of insulation—all this vanished. When Jane Weddell pressed her eyes to the fence now and looked down between the flowering weeds she saw an earth dark as loam.

Cabot Gunther rapped sharply on the translucent glass of Jane Weddell's studio door, a sound that announced he was about to, not might he, enter.

"Jane—there you are, busy in your very perfection."

She regarded him, smiling, wordless, not eager to put him at ease. He walked up close and leaned over her body to see what she was working on.

"Some of the Ediacaran fauna, yes?"

"Yes. They are remarkable, aren't they?" she answered, putting her eyes back to the microscope.

"Jane, I've a difficult thing to convey to you, which is why I've come down here instead of asking you to see me."

She turned to look at him. He found her composure annoying.

"The board met last night, to thrash out the budget. You're still on, I saw to that, but the feeling overall, is that this field"—here he indicated the stone before her—"is drying up, compared to others. The long and short of it is, you've created enough material for us. And since you actually take directions from other people—which periods to focus on, what to look for, and so on—and you yourself are not publishing, the board felt you'd see why we had to cut you back, to four days a week.

"Now, of course, you can still come in whenever you wish—and this will continue to be your office and no one else's—but I can only pay you now for four days a week. That would come out to your annual salary less two months'."

She ran the tips of her fingers lightly over her lips but did not say anything.

"I'm sorry. You know it's the ebb and flow of

money, Jane, whatever's new, hot. We've covered
this before. You could write your own ticket if you'd
only publish something, write more than notes, detailed descriptions, if you'd tackle the real meaning
of these things, present us with phylogenies and
ecologies."

"Would it be possible—"

"Benefits? The benefits package, all that—pen-
sion? Unchanged."

"Would you mind if I just went on the same way
but took two months off without pay?"

"No, it can't work that way. I have to reduce
each paycheck twenty percent. You'd in effect be
taking two months off with eighty percent of salary. Too much paid vacation, is what it would look
like."

She folded her hands under her chin and nodded
in polite, wry indignation.

"Don't pout, Jane. It doesn't become you," he
said.

"I'm not pouting, Cabe. I'm doing a sort of mathematics. In a few moments it will all seem possible."
She smiled at him. "Thank you."

"Make up whatever schedule you want for a week.
I'll make the adjustment in the payroll, you can handle
the hours, the vacation time, however you want."

He nodded curtly, affirming their agreement, and backed out the door, which he closed gently.

Later that summer, Jane Weddell started a notebook about the lot. She worked evening after evening, divesting her memory of all it held of this place from the afternoon she first saw it two years before, a few weeks after the building had been torn down. The more she demanded of her memory, the more it gave. The first notebook of two hundred pages gave way to a second, and she became aware in her notes of a pattern of replacement, of restored relationships. The incremental change was stunningly confirmed for her the morning she saw a black bear standing in the lot. She could not tell if it was male or female. It was broadside to her in the tall grass, chewing a white tuber. It lifted its head to the air for a scent, or perhaps it was only bothered by grass tickling its chin. She watched until it ambled on toward the gray fence at the back, which it appeared to wander through.

For the first time Jane Weddell decided to change her routing to and from the museum, even though by no longer walking certain streets regularly she knew she would begin to lose her sense of them. She wanted to know more about the open lot. She thought of it as a place she'd been searching for, a choice she was finally making, with which she was immediately at ease. The lot became a sort of companion, like friends she went to dinner with. She didn't press the acquaintance, any more than she did those of her friends. Only occasionally did she pause before the lot and stare for long minutes into its light and shadows. Early in the fall she saw a herd of deer, four does browsing and seeming to take no notice of her. That same morning she didn't notice until she was leaving a switching tail, a tawny panther hunkered in the tawny grass.

Winter came, but the grasses and wildflowers in the lot did not die back as they had the winter before. Every time Jane Weddell passed she would see animals. Even on the rawest days, when wind drove a dry, cold wall of air against her or when sleet fell, she would see foxes bounding. Flocks of chickadees. Sometimes she imagined she could hear a distant river. Other times she saw birds migrating overhead, through the buildings. The lot comforted her, and she puzzled over how she might return the comfort.

When winter was at its steadiest, in January, she went to Aruba with her sister's children. When she came back she saw instantly, the moment she turned the corner at Seventy-fifth Street, that it was gone.

She walked up the block slowly, wondering why she had not done something, whatever that might have been. A construction portico had been erected over the sidewalk. The chain-link fence was now woven with metal slats. She peered through a crevice where a fence post abutted the adjacent building. The lot was not there. A deep excavation faced her, with strands of twisted wire and pipe protruding from the pit's earthen walls. Fresh brick sat foursquare on pallets. Two crane buckets sat crookedly on the ground, half filled with rock and debris.

Jane Weddell stood before two plywood doors padlocked askew at the center of the fence and saw between their edges ten or twelve pigeons, drinking from a throw of rain puddles in the pit. Two workmen arrived in a red and silver pickup. One eyed her accusingly, warning her, as though she were a thief. She left. On the way to the museum she remembered a tray of samples she had set aside years before, rocks so vaguely fossiliferous even she was not sure anything could be drawn from them. So much of the fauna that existed on Earth between Ediacaran fauna in the Precambrian and the first hard-shelled creatures of Cambrian seas was too soft bodied to have left its trace. These rocks were of the right age, she knew, to have included some of these small beasts, and as she climbed the stairs to her studio she knew she was going to extract them, find them if they were in there. More than anything she wanted to coax these ghosts from their tombs, to array them adamantine and gleaming like diamonds below her windows, in shafts of sunlight falling over the city and piercing the thick walls of granite that surrounded her.

CONVERSATION

I t can't be said that I came here. Or that we talked about this. This is strictly friends, Essie. Old times' sake, you know? I've got a career on the line here."

"Your career's not in jeopardy on this, not the way you imagine it is. Besides, your true career is politics, not running Fish and Wildlife. I'm asking for something very simple. Put your hands to your soul on this one, Lewis. Take your soul up in your hands, tell me what you see."

"Cut the college talk."

"Ethics? A sense of the Beautiful? Did you leave all that behind in a bunch of essays in O'Rourke's class?"

"Essie, we're talking about the art of the possible here, we're talking politics. Reality."

"I'm sorry. I keep forgetting. Once you're inside the Beltway, language is just another technology."

"What does that mean?"

"I mean speak to me as my friend, not like someone paranoid about rumors. Like somebody who knows truth and integrity are *also* part of the art of the possible. Remember that guy?"

"What do you want from me?"

"I want you to face up like a man on this one."

"I'm not being a man here?"

"No, dammit, Lewis, you are not. You've lost a sense of family on this. You're maneuvering for position, for your own pleasure."

"Wait. Are we actually talking about Carol? Carol Gleason? Because that's *way* over."

"Oh, Lew. Wake up. This isn't sexual fidelity, it's your obsession with your *position*. 'Is she good-looking enough to be seen with me?' 'Can this guy hurt me?' 'Will this pay off for me?' You've come all this way, Lew—don't you remember what you said years ago about 'integrity'? About representing the voter, not just your career interests?"

"I represent the views of the American voter very well. No question. Look up the polls."

"Entertainers watch polls, Lew. Movie producers. This is your politics?"

"Essie, I respect your position. We're at an impasse here."

"What *is* my position?"

"You want me to unilaterally declare the ferruginous hawk endangered in the lower forty-eight."

"Not exactly. What I *want* from you has as much to do with our friendship as it does with the plight of that bird. I want you to *read* the reports; and then stand up and say to yourself, 'I did not go to Jefferson City, Missouri, to represent the people of the Thirty-ninth District, shake all those hands, make all those promises and become Speaker of the House, I did not serve all those tedious years in committees and on the stump for my party, I did *not*, after four years as Attorney General of the State of Missouri, accept a presidential appointment to head the U.S. Fish and Wildlife Service, to read a set of reports that demonstrate beyond a reasonable doubt that the life of the ferruginous hawk is virtually finished in the lower forty-eight states, its biology *terminated*, to then step aside and say, "Ladies and gentlemen, far be it from me to tell you that no creature, large or small, beautiful or ugly, for which I have responsibility shall stand in the way of one *single* job. Far be it from *me* to say that I will not hesitate to spend the currency of this country's biological heritage in bills large and small to ensure that no job, no matter how venal, destructive, outdated, wasteful, self-aggrandizing, or demanding will be threatened." No, I didn't come all this way to say that. What I want to say is: Here's my Rubicon. The last rivet in the plane has popped for me. I'm standing this ground.' "

"Very moving, Essie. Really. But the American people don't buy it."

"They'd go for it, in a way to make your shoes spin."

"Our polls—sorry, I'm sorry, but polls are a solid political reality and they don't show that."

"They would, if you'd ask questions that don't play so cleverly on selfishness and fear."

"I know people hate it—forest after forest, animal after animal. I don't like it either—but the country's more diverse than just *biology*."

"That's the heart of the madness right there, Lew. You can't *eat* computer printout. You can't *breathe* 'upturn in the economy.' An animal is not a 'system component,' any more than it's a constituent. *That's* closer to the problem."

"The Secretary just won't hear of it."

"What's happened here is that after twenty-three years your compromise with mediocrity is nearly complete."

"There are no complaints that I've heard."

"In the circles you travel in, you're not likely to hear a discouraging word. That, too, is the art of politics."

"Essie, please. I'd like to do this. Truth. I know it's right. But it's not the time. The elections are four months away. It'll hold until we're on the other side. I can delay it."

"What you mean is, you don't have the courage."

"No. What I *mean* is, I *have* a distinguished legacy of good decisions because they were *timely*. I've come this far, dammit, because I *know* something about timing."

"We're not talking timing, Lew, we're talking guts. We're talking intelligence. We're talking about the big bottom line."

"And that is . . . ?"

"Biology."

"Are you seriously suggesting that if these last few ferruginous hawks in the Great Basin and Montana disappear, humanity will suffer anything more than a psychic wound?—and I'm not slighting that, I've lost animals I loved—but, geez, the biological future of *Homo sapiens* is not hanging in the *balance* here."

"Oh, but it is, Lew. And you're the man with the power to make the decision. Anyone whose neurons are still firing knows that if you *don't* make it, this executive power is worthless. Popcorn. People with an attention span longer than a nightly news story know our biology is unraveling in a *holocaust* of extinct species, unprecedented in the history of the planet. Loss of diversity is not like losing the family dog, Lew. The best minds we've got, the ones *outside* government and business—and even *those* people are now signing on—are saying no, the risk is too great. We *can't* throw all this material in the wastebasket and expect 'business and technology' to take up the slack. At best they can hand us a few decades of weedlots in which to enjoy 'economic security.' Can't you see where this is going? What makes me angry is you've become so devoted, so careful, with your career and you can't see where it's taking you."

"You know, Essie—I know you won't like this— but women always try to run this stunt. They rouse men to go out and 'wage the good fight,' do the morally right thing. But, really, they like the situation just fine. They like the advantages that come with just playing ball, not becoming hysterical about how humanity's doomed."

"What kind of person have you become? What the hell are you talking about?"

"I'm talking about *Lisa*, my kids, my family, my *first* family. I'm talking about you and David and *your* kids. All our friends and their kids. I'm talking about how people *live*, Essie. Do *you* fight the good fight at the risk of your job? No! You don't have a job."

"I don't believe this."

"The head of the Environmental Defense League. No paid salary, no benefits, no retirement, expenses out of your own pocket—where the hell would you be, really, without David's income?"

"For Christ's sake, Lew, this isn't about *income*."

"Yes, it *is*, because it's only *because* of David's income that you have the free time to run this organization—I'll be blunt—it's his income that makes your rise in social class possible. I wouldn't *be* here with you now if it was just old school ties. Like it or not, in the end, these people are right—it's about jobs. You want me to fight the good fight for you, for us? Take the same risks I do. Put your head on the line, just like I do."

"I'm a little lost here. If your responsibility is to your family, why don't you get a job where you won't have to compromise your integrity on a daily basis?"

"My integrity is not compromised here."

"If it's not, horses can fly."

"I'm a practical man, Essie, like most men."

"I thought—forgive me—that you were something special."

"Don't use female flattery with me."

"Lew, do you believe there's a difference between love and sex?"

"What do we mean here?"

"What it means to love—to accept in spite of flaws, not to judge, but to support, to give in instead of asking for more room all the time? Do you know this?"

"Yes."

"What do you love?"

"I love Lisa, I love the kids. I love my job. What do you want me to say? I love the Earth. That's my job, to love the Earth, to love *all* of creation, *including* humanity, and to protect it from threat."

"But you won't do this."

"See, you're just trying to get something out of me."

"No, Lewis, really. I want you to have something for your*self*. I'd like to see you do this in part because in doing it I think you'll find again what started you down this path all those years back, and it will do you good. And I think you'd be surprised politically. If you acted on this, you'd galvanize people, people disaffected with politics and politicians. Yes, I'd like to see the ferruginous hawk protected. I value it as

I value anything alive, from tulips to sharks. But if you pressed me to a wall, I'd say the reason I asked you to come out here, to talk to me, was because *you* are my family, because I love and care for you, because I want to fight on your behalf, because your failure to act would grieve me as your death would grieve me. Is this only a *woman* talking, Lew? Or are we talking about the human voice here? Are we talking about an ethics that doesn't know gender?"

"You're very persuasive, I must say."

"I know—you've got to go."

"Yes."

"You have a few days. Thanks for agreeing to talk. You know what this is really about. You'll make it your Rubicon or a Tippecanoe."

"Yes. I'll give you a call."

"I won't need a call. But I'd appreciate it."

"It'll be the right kind of call, Essie, I think."

"I hope it is. We're going to see, aren't we?"

PEARYLAND

I apologize for not being able to tell you the whole of this story. It begins at the airport at Søndre Strømfjord in Greenland and it happened to a man named Edward Bowman. He'd just come down from Pearyland, by way of Qânâq and Upernavik, then Nûk. About a hundred of us were waiting around for planes, his out to Copenhagen, with Søndre Strømfjord socked in. He'd been at the airport for six days; I'd been there just a few, with four Inuit friends from Clyde Inlet, on Baffin Island. In those

days—1972, just out of law school—I was working
with Canadian Eskimos, helping to solidify a political confederation with Eskimos in Greenland.

We were all standing by, long hours at the airport.
Some people went into town; but the notion that the
weather might suddenly clear for just a few minutes
and a plane take off kept most of us around, sleeping
in the lounges, eating at the restaurant, using the
phones.

Bowman was at work on a master's degree in wildlife biology at Iowa State, though by that time he may
have already abandoned the program. His thesis, I
remember well, had to do with something very new
then—taphonomy. He was looking, specifically, at
the way whitetail deer are taken apart by other animals after they die, how they're funneled back into
the ecological community—how bone mineral, for
example, goes back into the soil. How big animals
disappear. Expanding the study a little brought him
to Pearyland. He wanted to pursue in northern
Greenland some threads of what happens when large
animals die.

I should say here that Bowman wasn't eager to
talk, that he didn't feel compelled to tell this story.
He didn't avoid my questions, but he didn't volunteer
much beyond his simple answers. His disinclination
to talk was invariably polite, not unlike my Inuit

friends', whose patience I must have tried all those years ago with my carefully framed questions and youthful confidence.

Did he go up there just to look at dead animals? I asked him. In a cold place where carcasses decay very slowly? Partly, he said. But when he'd read what little had been written about the place, he said, his interests became more complicated. Pearyland is an arctic oasis, a place where many animals live despite the high latitude—caribou, wolves, arctic hares, weasels, small animals like voles and lemmings, and many birds, including snowy owls. Bowman said he'd tried to get grants to support a summer of study. Of course, he was very curious about the saprophytic food web, the tiny creatures that break down organic matter; but, also, no one understood much about Pearyland. It was remote, with a harsh climate and very difficult and expensive to get to.

No funder was enthusiastic about Bowman's study, or his curiosity. (He told me at one point that part of his trouble in applying for grants was that, after working with the deer carcasses in Iowa, he just had an instinct to go, but no clear, scientific purpose, no definite project, which finally presented the larger institutions with insurmountable problems.) Eventually, he was able to cobble together several small grants and to enlist the support of a foundation in Denmark, which enabled him to buy food and a good tent. For his travel north to Qânâq he was going to depend on hitching rides on available aircraft. With the last of his funds he'd charter a flight out of Qânâq for Brønlund Fjord in early July and then arrange for a pickup in mid-September. All of which he did.

When we met, the only cash he had was his return ticket to Copenhagen, but he was not worried. Somehow, he said, everything would work out.

Now, here is where it gets difficult for me. I've said Bowman, unlike most white men, seemed to have no strong need or urge to tell his story. And I couldn't force myself to probe very deeply, for reasons you'll see. So there could be—probably are— crucial elements here that were never revealed to me. It's strange to think about with a story like this, but you'll be just as I was—on your own. I can't help it.

What Bowman found at Brønlund Fjord in Pearyland was the land of the dead. The land of dead animals.

When he arrived, Bowman made a camp and started taking long walks, six- or seven-mile loops, east and west along the fjord and north into the flat hills, into the willow draws. The fjord stood to the

south—open water at 82° North in July, which surprised him; but that is the nature of arctic oases.
Summer comes earlier there than it does farther
south, and it lingers a bit longer. In winter it's rela-
tively warmer. Some days, Bowman said, he wore
only a T-shirt.

Bowman's treks brought him within sight of many
animals in the first few days, but he wasn't able to
get near them. And, a little to his wonder, not once
on these long walks did he come upon an animal
carcass, not even a piece of weathered bone.

The only thing he worried about, he told me, was
polar bears. He saw seals regularly in the fjord, so
he expected bears would turn up; but he saw no
tracks or scat, not even old sign. He wasn't afraid of
being attacked so much as of having a bear break
into his food. He had no radio, so he ran the risk of
starving before the plane came back. For this reason
alone, he said, he had agreed to take a gun, which
the Danish government insisted he carry. How he
learned where he was, that he'd camped in the land
of the dead, was that one morning he went for the
rifle and it wasn't there.

Of course, no one was around, so its loss made no
sense to him. He looked underneath everything in
his camp, thinking, absentminded, he might have

left it at his defecation pit, or taken it down to the shore of the fjord. Or that in his sleep he'd gotten up and taken the gun somewhere and thrown it away. He said he entertained this last possibility because he was never comfortable with the idea of having the gun; and who could know, he said to me, what the dreaming mind really wanted done?

The day after he missed the gun he saw a few caribou close by, less than a half mile away. He was eating breakfast, sitting on an equipment crate, watching the wind ripple the surface of the fjord and tracing with his eye a pattern in the purple flowers of a clump of saxifrage. The animals' hard stare caused him to turn around. He gazed back at them. Four animals, all motionless. It struck him then that in that first week or so he hadn't seen any caribou or muskoxen grazing or browsing.

He reached for his binoculars, but in that same moment the caribou dropped off behind a hill. He saw no other animals the rest of the day, but the following morning the caribou were back in the same place. This time, he sat very still for a long while. Eventually the caribou walked down to where he was, only about twenty yards away.

"Where is your place?"

Bowman said when he heard these words he thought it was the animals that had made them, but when he turned around he saw, far off near the edge of the water, a man, an Inuk.

"What place are you from?"

It was hard for Bowman to understand that this man's voice was coming to him clearly even though he was standing far away. He didn't know what to answer. He didn't think the man would know about Indiana, so he said he was from very, very far away, to the west and south.

"What do you want here?"

Bowman told me he wished to answer this question in such a way that he would not offend the man because he had a strong feeling he might be hindered in his study here (which, he pointed out again, was nearly aimless). Or possibly harmed.

"I want to listen," he said finally.

"Do you hear the wind? Meltwater trickling down to the fjord? The arctic poppies turning on their stalks in the summer sunshine?"

"Yes. I listen to all this."

"Do you hear the songs of my brothers and sisters?" asked the man by the fjord.

"I'm not sure," answered Bowman. "I don't think I've heard any singing. Perhaps if I listened better."

At that moment, Bowman turned quickly to look at the caribou. They'd come much closer. Swinging still further around, he caught sight of two wolverine, that odd lope of theirs, as they came bounding toward him from the west. Then the Inuk was right next to him, sitting on another crate, looking out over the waters of the fjord. Bowman couldn't make out his face from the side.

"I'm the caretaker here," the man said. Bowman could see now that he was about forty, fifty. "What do you want? What is 'Indiana'?" he asked.

Bowman, startled, described where Indiana was. Then he tried to explain what he did as a biologist, and that he was specifically interested in what happened to animals after they died. After that, he told me, he shouldn't have said anything more, but he went on until he ran out of things to say.

"The dead come here," the man said when Bowman was finished talking. He stood up. Bowman saw he was short, only five feet four inches or so, his short-fingered hands massive, the veins prominent, his forehead receding into a line of close-cropped, raven black hair. "You've come to the right place," he said. Then he walked away. Although he walked slowly, soon he was very far away.

The caribou were gone. The wolverine were still there, watching him, but after a while they, too, disappeared.

Bowman did not see the man again for four or five

days, and then he just saw him at a great distance, walking along the low edge of the sky.

One morning Bowman crawled out of his tent and saw an arctic fox resting on its haunches, looking at seals in the fjord. When he made a sound—his sock scraping on tundra gravel—the fox turned around quickly, surprised, and ran away. As he sprinted off, Bowman saw he had no shadow.

Bowman tried to arrange each day according to the same schedule. When he awoke, he took his binoculars and studied the tundra in every direction, writing down whatever he saw—arctic hare, muskoxen, snow geese. He ate, then took a lunch and his pack and went for a long walk. He made lists of all the flowers, the tracks he came upon, the animals he saw; and he fought against a feeling that he was not accomplishing anything. Every day he wrote down the temperature and he estimated the speed and direction of the wind and he made notes about the kind of clouds he saw in the sky. Altostratus. Cumulonimbus.

One day the man came back. "Why aren't you trying to hunt?" he asked. "How come you don't try?"

"When I was a young man I hunted with my father in Indiana. I don't do that now." Bowman told me he wanted to be very careful what he said. "I don't hunt here, in this place, because I brought food with me. Besides, I don't know these animals. I have no relations with them. I wouldn't know how to hunt them."

"No hunting here, anyway."

"I know this is your country," Bowman said cautiously, "but why are you here?"

"Caretaker. Until these animal spirits get bodies and are ready to go back, a human being must be here, to make sure they aren't hungry. If the animals want something—if they want to hear a song, I learn it. I sing it. Whatever they want, I do that. That's my work."

"Have you been here a long time?"

"Yes. Long time. Soon, someone else will come. A long time ago, before Indiana, there was more work. Many caretakers. Now, fewer."

"What do these animals eat?"

"Eating—it's not necessary." After a moment he said, "They are feeding on the sunlight."

"When they are ready, where do they go?"

"All everywhere. They go home. They go back where they're from. But too many, now, they don't come here. They are just killed, you know. No prayer." He made a motion with his fist toward the ground as though he were swinging a hammer. "They can't get back there then. Not that way."

"Which ones come back?"

The man regarded Bowman for a long moment. "Only when that gift is completed. Only when the hunter prays. That's the only way for the animal's spirit to get back here."

"Do they come here to rest?"

The man looked at Bowman strangely, as if Bowman were mocking him with ignorant questions. "They get their bodies here."

"But only if they are able to give their lives away in a certain manner, and if the hunter then says a prayer?"

"Yes."

After a while the man said, "Many religions have no animals. Harder for animals now. They're still trying."

Bowman did not know what to say.

"Very difficult, now," said the man.

"What do you hear in this place?" the Inuk asked abruptly. "Do you hear their songs? Do you hear them crying out?"

"In my sleep," Bowman ventured. "Or perhaps when I am awake but believe I'm sleeping. I hear a sound like a river going over a wall, or wind blowing hard in the crown of a forest. Sometimes I hear heartbeats, many heartbeats overlapping, like caribou hooves."

"The souls of the animals calling out for bodies, bodies calling out for their souls."

"The bodies and the souls, searching."

"Yes. They come together, falling in love again like that. They go back, have children. Then one day someone is hungry, someone who loves his family, who behaves that way. Wolf, human being—the same. That's how everything works."

"Is there another place," asked Bowman, "where the animal souls go if they are just killed?"

The Inuk looked at Bowman as if he weren't there and got up and walked away.

He didn't come back and Bowman didn't see him again.

The animals around Bowman's camp grew less shy. They began to move past him as though he were growing in the ground or part of the sky. The caribou all walked in the same, floating way, some pairs of eyes gleaming, some opaque, looking at the plants and lichens, at the clouds, and staring at rivulets of water moving across the tundra.

Bowman saw his gun one morning, leaning against a crate.

During his last days, he said, he tried to sketch the land. I saw the drawings—all pastels, watercolors, with some small, brilliant patches of red, purple, and yellow: flowers, dwarf willow, bearberry. The land was immense. It seemed to run up against the horizon like a wave. And yet it appeared weightless, as if it could have been canted sideways by air soft as birds breathing.

The pilot came and took him out to Qânâq, nearly five hundred miles. Two days later he began traveling south. Now, with the rest of us, he was waiting for the weather to clear.

Bowman told me this story over three days. He said it only a little at a time, as though he were not certain of it or me. I kept trying to get him to come back to it, but I wasn't insistent, not rude. I had many questions. Did the animals make sounds when their feet touched the ground? Did he see airplanes fly-ing over? Was he afraid ever? What was the Inuk wearing?

The hardest question, for I had no other reason than my own inquisitiveness to pursue him, was asking whether he had an address where I might reach him. He gave me an address in Ames, where the university is, but by the time I wrote he'd moved away; and like so many young people—he was twenty-three, twenty-four—he did not leave a for-warding address.

Sometimes when I am in a library I look up his name. But as far as I know he never wrote anything about this, or anything else.

The last day of September the fog lifted suddenly, as though it had to go elsewhere. Bowman's plane, which had been there on the ground for eight days, left for Copenhagen and an hour later I flew with my friends back to Frobisher Bay, on Baffin Island.

THE

NEGRO

IN

THE

KITCHEN

My daily routine is set. Each morning at sunrise—I can determine time of sunrise to within a
minute for my latitude and longitude—I'm up and
into the shower. Then I prepare a fresh breakfast
which I vary meticulously, according to a strict,
weekly schedule. (In my reading on human evolution
and in my studies of debilitating human disease, I
have seen consistent evidence that a lack of seasonal
variety brings on poor health. It predisposes one to
a whole range of cancers, to chronic fatigue, and

early death. My diet, therefore, is both precisely
matched to change of climate at my latitude—44°
North—*and* perfectly suited to my body, a biochem-
istry known to me in detail thanks to a long-term
series of tests at the Scripps Clinic—for traces of
heavy metals in the fingernails, seasonal fluctuation
in the concentration of melanin, that sort of thing.)

So I begin each day with the very reasonable coor-
dinate of local sunrise and, weather permitting, have
my breakfast on a wide porch overlooking the Wood
River, whose moods often calm me, particularly if
it's been a night of bad dreams.

My wife, a very undisciplined woman, ran off
several years ago. Our children, three of them, have
lives of their own but I'm in touch with them regularly. My companions are three Siamese cats—of the
not-so-common Vera Cruz strain—and a purebred
Akita, which I've raised from puppyhood and who
has a pile of blue ribbons. (We run twelve miles a
week.)

On the morning I wish to speak of, I entered the
kitchen at a little after six and saw a large Negro
standing there, a man dressed in baggy khaki shorts
and a plain but rather threadbare long-sleeved shirt.
Resting on the floor near him was a not-very-large
leather shoulder satchel. He had his back to me at

the open porch door and said without turning around, "I've set a second place—I hope you don't mind."

Well, I thought, how am I going to mind? Besides, he looked robustly healthy, even refined. The dog hadn't barked and even now wasn't disturbed by him. He was standing by his bowl waiting for his spring water. So I said, "No, fine. It's fine. I can prepare two portions—but you'll have to eat what I eat."

He seemed uninclined to speak but in some sort of reverie, staring off into the quaking aspen and the cottonwoods. I made fresh orange juice, lightly toasted two slices of bran bread, dished out my own yogurt for each of us, and served on the porch with Kenyan coffee—none of the South or Central American beans are good for me.

We began eating in silence. His table manners were good. Why had he come in? Would he attempt to push his way further into the house now? Would he ask to use the shower? When had he *entered* the house? I gave away nothing of my apprehension, but wondered if I should mention, of course, my schedule, a need to be at the office by seven.

"I never lock up, you know," I said. "Where did you come from?"

"I came from Connecticut. Greenwich. I have a business there . . . financial consultation."

"But—you're visiting here? Are you lost?"

"No, no, I'm walking. I'm taking a long walk. I *walked* here from Connecticut."

"But that's two thousand miles!"

"Yes, exactly. A very long way. I've been walking through the countryside most of the time, off the roads, eating fruits and nuts from orchards, garden vegetables—and depending on the hospitality of people such as yourself, for which I'm most grateful.

"I have read, in fact, some good books about 'living off the land,' " he said, reaching for his satchel, "one of which is exceptional. Do you know this?" He showed me the cover. No. "I never knew anything about this sort of thing when I was growing up. I grew up in Boston, we were the black bourgeoisie, you know. My father was a lawyer. We never did anything like this."

"Would you like another slice of toast? I make only one for myself. And I can actually, now, offer you some papaw marmalade—which I won't use until Thursday. I keep to a strict diet—to stay fit."

"Yes. Thank you."

"So," I ventured, waiting for the toast to pop back. "From here you will just be on your way?"

"That's right. Are you thinking I might steal the television?" He inclined his head toward the little seventeen-inch I use only for the news.

"It's perhaps not quite as absurd as you think," I countered. "Who are you, anyway? A stranger who shows up in my kitchen—large—and let's be frank—black." I wanted to be firm but not testy, and I was.

"About a year ago," he answered, spreading the marmalade on his toast (but directly from the jar), "I decided I wanted to see what lay west of Connecticut. As a boy I traveled everywhere in Europe. I finished a degree in history at the Sorbonne—yes. I taught in Kinshasa for a year, a disaster that saddened me for months after. I returned to the States, finished an MBA at Penn—Wharton. A year on Wall Street—among, I must say, some of the worst people I've ever known: lethal, pathologically selfish. That drove me to set up private practice in Greenwich, where I've done well. I have a gift for investing."

"I'm an investment counselor, right here in Sun Valley. That's exactly what I do. I'm a whiz at it, too."

"But I had never been off for any length of time in the country—not wilderness, not suburbia or exurbia but the countryside. I should have been curious, you know, about inner-city blacks, even guilt-ridden perhaps; but I wasn't. About five years ago—just try to imagine this—I started reading popular books about American Indians: *Bury My Heart at*

Wounded Knee. The Man Who Killed the Deer. Black Elk Speaks. I thought it was all a bit strange—out of touch, you know. But the more I read the more I got caught up in something. I don't know how to describe what happened. I felt exhilaration. Transcendence. I felt suddenly reconnected."

"Let me make you some more coffee."

"Thank you. So I went to Kenya. My ancestors were Kikuyu, hauled out to Zanzibar by Arabs in the 1840s. I looked into that history—Myungu, Songoro in Mwanza, Simba in the Congo. The names probably mean nothing to you, but these people were ferocious fighters, dreaded by every Arab slaver. I admired them terrifically; but whatever it was I was after in Africa—the famous roots, a sense of identity—I never found it. I went home. I decided this African direction was unprofitable for me. The place I loved, the place I was truly part of, was so obviously the Connecticut River Valley. I had known this as a boy—my parents had a house there. My *own* children—I have two, a boy nine, a girl twelve—love that place. My wife as well. Why was I trying to find some place in Africa?"

"I don't actually have to leave for work. Do you mind, I might have another toast?"

"Certainly."

From where I was standing in the kitchen I could

just see my visitor's head above the countertop, past the French doors. His index fingers were braced against his pursed lips. He moved his hands beautifully. I wondered if he had been successful in sports.

"I'm quite taken with this story of yours," I declared, sitting back down and studying for a moment the way light was shimmering on the surface of the river.

"You're interested. But you don't know what to make of it. An educated black, an income probably comparable to your own. Probably even a politics not much different from your own. Disturbing."

"Well, whatever you're doing out there in the woods, you seem determined to make something of yourself. *That's* admirable."

"My life was handed to me." He caught my eye. "True for you?" I didn't answer. "I went to good schools, I met no resistance getting what I wanted. In France I was even less frequently confronted by racism. But that was not enough. All I had read about Indians before I went to Africa stayed with me. I started in again, my strange attraction; only this time it struck me in a very different way. I wanted to become an African-American indigene."

"And what is that?"

"A black man who identifies with the American landscape, who fractures the immorality of his heritage in this country so completely that he finally gains a consoling intimacy with the place, the very place that for so long had been unapproachable. I had always imagined the hills, the rivers, the sky regarding us the way the whites did, as interlopers. Because I thought whites owned the land, that they were the same. We were strangers, whose inquiries, whose desire for companionship, were not welcome."

I reached blindly for my Peterson's *Field Guide* on the window ledge. "That small bird that just flew by—excuse me—I need to identify it. I have only nine birds to go, then I will have seen every one that lives in this valley. And yes . . . please, yes, I am listening—but here it is: Solitary vireo. Wonderful. Go ahead. Wonderful."

"I needed to see the breadth of the land. To be in it. To hold it and be held by it."

"Yes. I see. You may not think this relates to what you're doing, but I grew up in Bel Air and I needed to see the land, which is why I built this house."

"So, about seven months ago, I left Connecticut and started walking toward the Pacific. I stayed far away from cities, lived as much as I could off the land, wild land and domesticated land. I could, right now, walk into those aspens, take one of those stones there by the river, cut a shaft, harden it, and put venison on your table before noon. I can do that—

but in no way am I adverse to this delicious yogurt, to your bread and oranges. This is Kenyan, isn't it?" I nodded yes.

"My desire," he continued, "took this focus: to travel intimately across the country, to flow beautifully over the land, making very little disturbance, until I stood on the rim of the Pacific. I've taught myself all sorts of things in this process. I can now go three or four days without food. I can imitate the songs of almost two hundred birds—that was a female Ruby-crowned kinglet, by the way, not a Solitary vireo—"

"Damn, I've got that."

"—and travel nearly as fast in the dark as I can in daylight. I set myself the task, for example, of crossing Iowa in just ten days, traveling more than thirty miles a night, without being seen. Not so much as one dog barked. In Wyoming, I stayed for a short time with the Crow, a very interesting kind of people. Custer had Crow scouts, you know. They and the Arikara were the only tribes in the West who decided it was pointless to fight white people. When my boy is older, I'm going to send him to live with the Crow."

"We had Indians in my family. My mother was one-eighth Comanche. I'm one-sixteenth."

"Only a few hundred miles to go now. Another few weeks and I'll reach the Pacific. I want to taste western salmon, learn to discriminate if I can among the flesh of silver, chinook, sockeye, and pink salmon. See if the nuts from chinquapin trees are bitter."

"What do you do for money?"

"I said, an investor."

"No, now."

"I don't need money now. Not much. At the start I was apprehensive, traveling without cash, no credit cards. But after a while, really, the whole issue faded."

"Because I want to give you a hundred dollars. Two hundred, actually, just in case."

"It's very kind of you but—"

"No, no. I admire what you're doing. I want to support it."

He searched my face. "Have you ever thought, yourself," he said, "of going out there? Of just walking away from this house, your business?"

"I do. Every winter. I go to Eleuthera in the Bahamas. I have a house. I dive. I know all the species of fish."

"Think about this—I know you can see this: the white man's jobs kept most blacks in the cities. He closed Indians up on the reservations. He wasn't comfortable with either of us traveling around. He believed blacks had some sort of bush voodoo, and that Indians had another sort of voodoo, and it would be best if Indians just stayed on the reservations and if blacks just worked hard in the factories, making cars and cotton sheets. We have lived apart from all that. You know when I run—those hours on end across the fields in Iowa—I recite the *Aeneid* to myself? Yes. I love that story. *Sic fatur lacrimans, classique immittit habenas . . .* that's the beginning of the sixth book, the middle of the story. Or the poetry of Wallace Stevens. Do you believe that? I glide the land, the river bottoms, the mountain parks, with that music in my head."

"I *have* thought about leaving, just throwing it all in."

"You must find something that really drives you. It has to be more than just an idea."

"A commitment."

"Deeper."

"Binding contract."

"A contract, yes—but with your *heart*, not your head."

"Quite the step."

"Exhilarating!"

"Did you find it hard, memorizing all the birdsongs?"

"The birdsongs? Yes. That was hard, but each task you will find is very sweet, sweet to recall."

"I see. Sweet to recall . . . I'm—so, do you just take off now? Can I give you a lift? Should I even offer to give you a lift?"

"Very kind, and thank you, but no." He straightened the silverware on his plate. "See those cottonwoods? I'm going to go over there now and just disappear in them. Make for Galena Pass, then over into Stanley Basin tonight."

"How do you find the places to sleep?"

"Some things remain a mystery, even to me."

"Those Nike crosstrainers. They're good?"

"My shoes? These shoes? Why, yes, they're good."

"If I went, do you think I should run to the *Atlantic*? What are you going to do when you reach the Pacific?"

"The Pacific?" He looked at me closely, a long look. Perhaps he was sizing me up as a traveling companion. "I might wonder, really, whether I'd earned it."

"Earned it? Of course you have!" How could he doubt it?

He pushed his chair back. "Let me do these," he said.

When he stood up to take the dishes, I was surprised, again, by his size. He reminded me of a professional basketball player whose name I couldn't then think of.

I pointed him to the guest bathroom on my way past the sink, then went to my bedroom and took two hundred dollars out of my wallet and returned to the kitchen. He was rinsing the dishes and setting them on the drainboard, where they shone in the sunlight.

I handed him the two hundred-dollar bills. He accepted them but with a peculiar smile. I asked him if he wanted any food. He led us out through the French doors and leaned over the table to take a nectarine from a large bowl of fruit.

"Will I see you again?"

"No, I doubt we will meet again."

I knew he wanted to leave, but I didn't want the conversation to end. I'd never had such a long conversation with a Negro before.

"Well," I said with a shrug, "whoever heard of coming into the kitchen one morning and finding a huge black man standing there, someone who just ran out of the woods and wanted breakfast and then ran off again, like an Indian?"

"It's probably happened before, and it will likely happen again."

He reached down to pat the dog, who the whole time had been sleeping in the sun on the porch, very unlike himself. And then he waved and was just down the stairs, wading the strong, shallow river and gone into the woods.

I stood at the porch railing for a long time. I grew annoyed. I got my binoculars and put on another cup of coffee, which I never do after breakfast, and got down Arthur Cleveland Bent's *Thrushes, Kinglets, and Their Allies* and began reading the paragraphs on the Ruby-crowned kinglet.

THE
ENTREATY
OF THE
WIIDEEMA

I should preface my remarks this evening—and I must say that this will not be an entirely hopeful talk, and for that I apologize—with some explanations of how I came to live with—to try to live with, really— the Wiideema.

When I finished my doctoral studies among the Navajo of the American Southwest, I realized, as many students do, that I knew less at the end than I did in the beginning. That is, so much of what I took to be the objective truth when I started—things as self-evident, say, as Copernicus's arrangement of the inner planets—became so diluted by being steeped in another epistemology that simultaneously I came to grasp the poverty of my own ideas and the eternity of paradox within Navajo thought.

Let me put this to you in another way. When I finished my work among the Navajo—or, to be both more precise and more honest, when I gave up among the Navajo—I had as my deepest wish that someone among them would have been studying my way of knowing the world. I might have been more capable then of accepting the Navajo as true intellectual companions, and not, as has happened to so many of us, have ended up feeling disillusionment, even despair, with my own culture. I believe I would have been able to grasp *our* expression of Beauty Way, and in that sense I would have fallen back in love with my own people.

But it did not work this way. My postdoctoral studies brought me here, to Austin, where I declared I wanted to look at something I'd never studied before—among people I'd have to go out and *find*, an undiscovered people. On the strength of my work with the Navajo—and, again, to be candid with you, although I learned to speak that extremely difficult language fluently and though, for example, I memorized the full nine days of Blessing Way prayers, the obsession cost me my marriage, my two children—on the strength of that earlier work, I was granted awards and fellowships by the Wenner-Gren Foundation, the Kellogg Foundation, the University of Texas at Austin, and the Henry Solomon Memorial Trust. This financial support, and the regard with which my own department treated me—my teaching duties here were light to begin with, and I must acknowledge, embarrassing as it is, that I *took* them lightly—with all this underpinning, I set out to find a tribe of people with whom I could explore one idea—hunting.

The conventional wisdom on this, of course, is that there are no intact hunting cultures left in the wilder Southern Hemisphere—not in Africa, not in South America, not in Australia. I'd learned through a friend, however, that it was possible a few, small hunting bands might still exist uncontacted in the Western Desert, in Australia. So I went there immediately. I'll be brief about this part of it. An important question—Why disturb these people if they are, indeed, there?—was one I deliberately ignored. I suppressed it, I will tell you, with a terrible intellectual strength. I importuned every professional acquaintance, until I got myself so well situated in the anthropological community I was able to arrange a small expedition, with the approval of the Central

(Aboriginal) Land Council, into a region of Western Australia west of the Tanami Desert, where I was most hopeful of contacting a relict hunting band. It is now safe, though still compromising, to reveal that I lied to arrange this expedition, both to my friends and to the Land Council. I was not interested, as I claimed, in searching out the last refuges of rare marsupial animals and in comparing what I could learn of their biology and ecology with information gathered in conversations with local people and gleaned from scholarly publications on their hunting practices, belief systems, myths. I wanted to find a fresh people, and to pursue with them another idea.

When the Wiideema, in fact, found *us*—in the Northern Territory, technically, not in Western Australia, though the designation of course meant nothing to them—I was ecstatic. As soon as I realized the Wiideema were shadowing us—a fact I was the last to discover, though I believed I was the first— I contrived to abandon my white companions and our aboriginal guides. Under cover of darkness one night I simply walked out of camp. I'd not gone but a mile before I felt the presence, the subtle pressure, of other people. And there they were, standing like so many dark sticks in the sand among tufts of spinifex grass. Truly, it was as though they had materialized.

I made signs that I very much wished to join them

and leave my companions. We walked that night until I was delirious with exhaustion. We slept the whole of the next day in the shade of some boulders, walked all the following night, and then did the same again, another two days. My exhaustion turned to impatience, impatience to anger, anger to despair, and despair to acquiescence. In this manner I was bled.

Through it all I took notes, most especially on hunting. My position during those first few weeks, however, could be construed as that of a camp dog. I was given scraps to eat, patted on the shoulder by some of the older women, was yelled at, and served as a source of laughter when performing ordinary tasks—making a double-secure tie in the laces of my boots, for example, or when I examined the binding on a spear shaft with a hand lens.

One day, having had more than my fill of this and being the butt of pranks—the children sniped at me in the same way their parents did, a probing but ultimately indifferent curiosity—I confronted one of the men, Karratumanta, and with a look of defiant exasperation burned a smoking hole in a eucalyptus limb with my hand glass. Karratumanta regarded me blankly. He picked up a stone and threw it with terrific force at a small bird flying by. The stone knocked the bird, a songlark, to the ground, dead.

He stripped away and ate its two minute slabs of pectoral flesh and then regarded me as though I were crazy to assume superiority.

You can imagine how this played out, certainly, in those first weeks. On reflection, I realized my plans had probably been transparent to my white companions and to our guides, and that they had no intention at all of searching for me. Instead, they trusted little harm and some good would come from my conceits and lack of integrity. I hope, in the end, you will find that they were correct.

In the early days of my work with the Wiideema— I call it "my work" because it was work, keeping up with them—I was dazzled, predictably, by the startling degree of their intimacy with the places we traveled through. The capacity of every object, from a mountain range to an insect gall, to hold an idea or to abet human life was known to them. I expected this high level of integration with place, a degree of belonging that the modern world envies, perhaps too desperately; but I was not prepared for the day I began to hear English words in their conversations. The first words I heard were "diptych," "quixotic," and "effervesce," words sufficiently obscure to have seemed Wiideema expressions, accented and set off in the run of conversation exactly as they would be in English. But they were not Wiideema words. Over a period of days I began to hear more and more English, not just words but phrases and occasionally entire sentences. What was happening was so strange that I did not want to ask about it. During my years in the field, if I have learned one thing, it is not to ask the obvious question right away. Wait, and you often see the whole event more clearly.

When I could understand almost everything that was being said, though in a way I'd never understood English before, I asked Yumbultjaturra, one of the women, "Where did you learn to speak English?"

"What is that, 'English,' the name of your language?"

"It's what we're speaking."

"No, no," she said smiling. "We are merely speaking. You, *you*, I think, might be speaking that."

"But we can understand each other. How could we understand each other if we both weren't speaking English?"

"We can understand each other because—how should I put this to you?—we do not have a foreign language. You understand what I say, don't you?"

"Yes."

"At first you didn't."

"Right, yes."

"However," she said, "from the beginning we understood you."

"From the start? Then why did you never answer my questions, why didn't you speak to me?"

"We spoke to you all the time," she stated. "And forgive me, but your questions were not compelling. And to be truthful, no one was inclined to speak with you until you put your questions away. You'd have to say this is a strict tenet with us—listening."

Our conversation went on in this manner for five or ten minutes before I understood what she was doing. She wasn't, in fact, speaking English. It was not even correct to say that she was speaking Wiideema. She was just speaking, the way a bird speaks or a creek, as a fish speaks or wind rushes in the grass. If I became anxious listening to her, she got harder to understand. The more I tried to grapple with our circumstances, the less I was able to converse. Eventually, in order to understand and be understood, I simply accepted the fact that we could understand each other.

Now, knowing this, I can imagine what you are perhaps anticipating—but it did not happen. I had no intellectual discussion with the people I traveled with. We did not discuss or compare cosmologies. I did not seek to discover whether the grand metaphors

of my own culture—entropy, let us say, or the con-
cept of husbandry—had their counterparts in Wiideema culture. I did not pursue any philosophical
issues with them, say Gandhi's ahimsa, or the possibility of universal justice. No Enlightenment notions
of universal human dignity. I simply traveled. I drew
the country into myself, very much as I drew air into
my lungs. Or drank water. I ceased what finally
seemed to me my infernal questions and menacing
curiosity. And I finally came to see the Wiideema as
a version of something of which my own people were
a version. What we shared—and it was a source of
pleasure as intense as any I had ever known—was
not solely food and a common hearth, human touch,
small gifts, things I would have expected, but a sense
of danger. A sense that it was dangerous to be alive.

I do not mean by such danger poisonous snakes
or no water; or solely that you might be bludgeoned
in your sleep, all of which occurred. The sense of
danger we shared came from accepting consciousness. Human consciousness beckons us all. My Wiideema companions, wary as wild animals, had not
accepted it fully. They didn't shun knowledge; and
it was not that they were never contemplative or
curious about ideas or other abstractions. But their
hesitancy had led them off in another direction. All
that they knew, all they believed or imagined, they

cast in stories. Stories for them were the only safe containers for what consciousness, as we have it, might have elucidated for them about life. Or let me say this another way. When I put my imagination, as distinct from my intellect, together with their stories, having steeped my body in the food, the water, light, wind, and sand of the Wiideema, I found as much in these stories as I could expect to find in the most profound and beautiful Occidental articulation of any idea or event with which I am familiar.

I finally left the Wiideema—a decision awful and hard to arrive at—because I could not exercise the indifference they managed toward violence. On several occasions, the fourteen people I traveled with encountered other groups. Often these encounters were friendly, but three times they were fatally violent. Someone was murdered. And then life started over again. In a troubling way this was like hunting. An animal was killed and eaten, and all were refreshed. The distinction, the emotional and moral separation between human and animal death, was one I could never grasp in my Occidental mind and not perceive in my infant Wiideema mind. They were willing to accept far more suffering in their lives— from heat, from starvation, from thirst, from wounds—than I could abide. And nothing but thoughts of retribution, as far as I knew, were raised for them by incidents of murder.

In the end, I did not consider that the Wiideema lived on some lower plane, or, transcendent in their infinitely clever world of stories, that they lived on a higher plane. I thought of them as companions on the same plane, shielding themselves in a different way from the fatal paradoxes of life.

When I left the Wiideema it was in the same fashion as I had arrived, rising in the night and walking away, though I understood now this was only a ritual, that my departure was not camouflaged. I had learned enough to get on alone in the desert, unless circumstances became truly dire. I walked out at Yinapaka, a perennial lake in the outwash of the Lander River, and eventually met some Warlpiri people who took me to Willowra. From there I came home.

What I hoped to find when I left Austin 2½ years ago was an uncontacted people with whom I could study the hunting of animals. I was curious about how, emotionally and spiritually—if you will allow me that imprecise word—people accustom themselves to daily killing, to the constant taking of life, as I saw it. I was afraid that in my dealings with the

Navajo, a people studied nearly to death, all I was learning was a version of what I or others already knew. What I found when I began to travel with the Wiideema was that their emotions, their spiritual nature, was unknowable. When we killed and roasted kangaroo, I could only inquire into my own ethics, question my own emotions. I sought, finally, companionship with the Wiideema, not reason, not explanation.

I have to say, however odd it may sound, that what little true knowledge I returned with is knowledge already known to us—that we and the Wiideema share the same insoluble difficulties, which each day we must abide. And that not "once" but *now* is a time when human beings all speak the same language. (What actually happens, I think, is that people simply speak their own language but it is clearly understood by each listener.)

I wanted, 2½ years ago, to gain another kind of knowledge, the wisdom, so named, of primitive people. One day my friend Karratumanta killed a man called Ketjimidji. He speared him quickly through the lungs without warning. There were six or seven of us standing together when it happened. We had met on a trail, Ketjimidji's people coming from a soak or water hole and our group walking toward it. No voices were raised. No argument broke out. The killing—Karratumanta handled Ketjimidji deftly, coolly, on the spear, until Ketjimidji went down and stopped struggling—was followed by a preternatural silence. Ketjimidji's people went away, carrying the body with them, and we walked ahead to the soak. In the moments right after the killing I was fine but soon I was fighting for air. I felt as if all the bones in my face had exploded.

Ngatijimpa, one of Karratumanta's daughters, came to me that night and told me a story. It had nothing to do, as far as I could see, with what had happened. It was one of a long series of stories about the travels of Pakuru, the golden bandicoot. She was not, I finally understood, offering me allegory or explanation, but only a story, which, as she intended, pulled the sense of horror out of me in some mysterious way. I slept. But I remembered. And my nights afterward were disturbed because I remembered. I couldn't be healed of it, if that is the right word.

Karratumanta, a tutor of mine, had seen me reeling after the spearing and said, "I will not be your martyr."

Many months later I was spattered by blood when another person was killed violently in front of me. Again, Ngatijimpa came to me. She told me another part of the story of Pakuru and his travels and under the soothe of the story I slept deeply. Ngatijimpa was young, only a girl, but she was eloquent and effective with the wisdom she dispensed.

I owe those who have supported me an exact and detailed report of my months with the Wiideema, a scholarly work rigorous in its observations, well researched, cautious in its conclusions. I have begun this paper, and, somewhat to my surprise, I have made progress. In it I'm describing hunting techniques, the ethology of desert animals; but what I am really wondering, night and day, is what I can give the Wiideema. Such questions of allegiance seize upon us all I believe—how can we reciprocate, and how do we honor the unspoken request of our companions to speak the truth? What I wish to do here, the task-in-return I have set myself, is to rewrite the story of Cain. I want to find a language for it that offers hope in place of condemnation, that turns not on aggression and vengeance, but on the mystery of human terror.

I do not know if I will be successful, or—if I am—whether success will mean anything substantial. But having sojourned with the Wiideema, I want to understand now what it means to provide.

HOMECOMING

Oh, Maddy. He almost spoke aloud. The girl was squatting by wild irises, examining them as though she expected them to speak. In that moment he loved her very much and felt the burden of his absences like stone piled upon his back. She ran impatiently ahead. "Madelon, Madelon," he murmured, his heart graying with self-reproach.

In the fall of 1985, on the basis of a single paper in the *International Journal of Tropical Plant Ecology,*

Wick Colter achieved a level of international status few of his teachers—and no fellow graduate student—had known. He had anticipated the reaction, and he accepted congratulations from his colleagues with rehearsed graciousness, fearful lest he seem foolishly enthusiastic about his own work. The paper's publication resulted in a growing stream of invitations to lecture and consult, some prestigious and many of them lucrative.

Colter's fortunate path—when he finished a Ph.D. at Oregon State he was offered and took a position on the faculty; with his lecture and consultation fees he was able to double his salary; his wife's parents helped them buy twenty-four acres on the Calapooia River in the foothills of the Cascades—this path to good fortune for Colter began accidentally. He'd called on a botany professor one morning and was scanning her shelves for a book when the professor's phone rang. It was a student at another school, phoning to say she had to drop out of a field trip scheduled to depart in four days for Peru. When she hung up, the professor asked, almost perfunctorily, if Colter wanted to take the student's place. He said yes, though he had no compelling reason to go. He described it later as intuition.

Colter assembled a research project in a couple of days, bought and borrowed personal gear, and left on time with the others. They flew to Lima, then to Pucallpa on the Rio Ucayali. From the river they headed into the jungle, to a region near the Brazilian border. Colter spent three weeks collecting plants in the family Comistelliacae, many of them in the genus *Ellox*. He had been told that Comistelliacae was a confused family, that its taxonomy would benefit greatly from the attention of even such a provisional plant evolutionist as himself.

Colter collected with a thoroughness and concentration, and with a tirelessness, the other graduate students found intimidating. When he returned to Oregon State, Colter immediately wrote to every scientist who had written about the evolutionary biology of Comistelliacae. He learned three botanists were just then finishing revised descriptions of three separate genera in Comistelliacae; but none was aware the other two had completed their work, publication of all of which was imminent. Colter also heard back from two plant ecologists in Nigeria, whose revisions in the systematics of three separate families of plants in the parent order Rolandales were about to be published. Colter waited until all four of these articles were in print—one in a very obscure journal, and two of the three others in foreign journals— before he submitted his own paper to the *International Journal of Tropical Plant Ecology*.

Colter's suggested revisions of the single genus *Ellox* formed the core of his paper. In his concluding remarks, however, he drew together the work of the other five scientists to, in effect, redefine Comistelliacae, the family to which *Ellox* belonged. Much less forcefully, but very effectively, he redefined Rolandales, the order that contained and was dominated by Comistelliacae. It was a meticulous and intelligent paper, but would not have been nearly as important had Colter not benefited from the rare convergence of informative papers in his narrow field, and had not the other scientists done their work so well.

That Colter's article became famous for being a great piece of luck did nothing to compromise his scientific reputation—except among those who were jealous. To his credit, Colter continued to work energetically on the systematics of Rolandales, taking full advantage of the position he had been given.

In the months and years that followed publication of his paper, Colter traveled with increasing frequency. He made repeated collecting trips to Peru, to West Africa, to Indonesia. He flew to conferences in Europe, in South America, in Japan. He had not meant to neglect all else in his life; he felt compelled by the importance of his work and a growing awareness of his own influence. But, increment by increment, relations with his family began to slip; and his life at the university became attenuated. In defense, he would trade on his reputation, apologizing to his wife for his long and repeated absences, but insisting upon them; and begging off, again, on administrative responsibilities at the university.

When Madelon was born, Colter believed the child would fill the empty space he had created at home; when he understood how absurd this was he felt humiliated by his own stupidity, by the haste and shallowness of his thought. When his graduate students began interrupting his late night research at the herbarium, he realized the disturbances were the result of his own disregard, his rarely kept office hours.

Colter was not willing to change. He enjoyed the deference accorded him outside his home and away from the university, the favors extended to him by strangers. He felt guilt over the neglect of his students, at the shirking of his duty to serve on university committees; and a more intractable guilt knowing his daughter saw little of him and that the management of his home was left almost entirely to his wife. But he learned to ignore compunction, his culpability. Renowned at twenty-nine, he continued to hunt recognition.

. . .

"What's this, Daddy?" Madelon pointed to a cluster of pale lavender flowers.

"That's bittercress, honey. *Cardamine pulcherrima.*"

"And this, what's this?"

"That's . . ." He couldn't get the name. He had to think. Even then he wasn't sure. "That's miner's lettuce. It's *Claytonia perfoliata.* Can you say that, *Claytonia perfoliata?*"

The girl pronounced the words effortlessly.

They continued together on a trail through the woods, the girl yards ahead. He passed a cluster of skullcap, purple flowers that reminded him of lupine, but he could recall neither the popular nor the scientific name. On the way back to the house he brooded; it was clear he'd forgotten the names of half a dozen or more flowers that grew around his home. His mind, he realized, was attuned to the hundred categories and subcategories of Rolandales.

"Maddy," he called. "Here, take these to your mother." He held out a bouquet of Indian pinks.

"Mommy says we shouldn't pick flowers in the woods," said the girl diffidently.

"Well, Daddy's business is flowers, and Daddy knows what to pick and how to pick, so the flowers come back the next year. It's all right."

"We have flowers in the garden, Daddy."

"Take the flowers, Madelon. And give them to your mother."

"Yessir."

He felt reduced and imperious before the child. He wanted her forgiveness, for picking the flowers and for more, for his heedlessness.

The anger that was coming and going in Wick Colter caused people to avoid him. He interpreted their avoidance as disenchantment and he became more obsessive about his work, pursuing esoteric and eva-nescent lines of thinking solely in an effort to im-press. The papers based on this work did not pass peer review. He took the lack of endorsement as a sign of their disappointment in him, a measure in itself of his self-absorption. He began thinking less of advancement and more about a way out.

"I'm thinking about resigning," he said to his wife one night in bed.

"Resigning?"

"I've been doing a terrible job, just using the place, really, for the past two years. It's dishonest."

"Wick, if you're—"

"No, it's all right. I'm fine. I'm actually thinking about starting a new business with Terry Rademon. I've told you some about this. A few of these plants we're working on, they can be developed commercially for reforestation in Brazil."

She did not answer him. He felt the cold penetration of her doubt and the rickety scaffolding of his self-deception. He began again with her.

"You know the other day, out in the woods, I couldn't think of the names of half a dozen plants. Dumb. I felt like I haven't been in the woods in years."

"You haven't."

"Well, let's not let that get around."

"Don't be sarcastic. You haven't been out there. It's Maddy, now, who knows. She knows every plant that grows here. She asks you what they are to humor you."

"Thanks."

"What do you want from us, Wick?" She was angry and rolled over to face him. "We live here, you don't."

"This is my place, too," he said.

"It's just some place you occupy. Your life is out there somewhere, Djakarta or Manaus, or the herbarium. You don't know, don't understand, where you live anymore. All this prestige you have to have—what good is that to us? How does it help? How does your daughter benefit, knowing how ignorant her father is in his own woods? And if you say one word about your income I'll sock you."

"I understand, Alice. Believe me, I see what you mean."

"Do you? Do you see that you have traded in the love of your daughter, for this *thing*, this authority of yours? It's the center of your life—not Madelon, not me, not your home."

"I don't think that's exactly what's happened. I'm anxious, you know, about these last few papers—"

"Listen to me. When you were young, growing up here, you could describe every plant in these woods. You could pick them out in the dark. In the dark! You remember the night we drove up Quartz Creek with the lights off? You named them all—pearly everlasting, fireweed, bull thistle. Coral bells. You knew by their shadows, how they dipped in the wind. You were *here* then. Now, you look around, it's not part of you anymore. Why should they remember you when you can't remember them?"

"What's that?"

"These plants. What grew up between you. It's *that* you trade on, it's *that* you've used to get where you are. What if it was in their power simply to forget you?"

"Are you being serious?"

"I'm very serious."

Colter lay quiet, listening to his breathing.

"I could not be more serious," she said, laying her arm across her forehead in exasperation.

In the silence that followed, Colter concentrated as he had not in years on unlatching a door that had kept him from entanglements, from harm. He felt as though he were trying to break through his own chest. He remembered Marilyn Webber. He had never told Alice. Nor about Janet Carson. He had spent a single night with each woman, that was all. He had not fallen in love, he would say to defend himself, but, later, it only made the sense of infidelity in him worse.

"Alice, do you know where Haskin is?"

"Haskin?"

"The flower book."

"It's in Madelon's room. It's in the stack of books on her table."

"I'll be back," he said. He pulled on his pants and shirt and put his shoes on, sockless. The spine of Haskin's *Wild Flowers of the Pacific Coast* gleamed in the reflection of the night-light on his daughter's small table. He knelt by her bed. "Please, Maddy. Forgive me," he whispered. He rose and went softly out of the room.

He sat at the kitchen table for a half hour, looking at the photographs and reading the descriptions and names of the flowers on the worn pages. He closed the book, took a flashlight from a kitchen drawer, and went out. The moon was full behind an overcast sky. The lawn was wet with dew. When his eyes adjusted, he took the path he'd walked with his daughter days earlier. The first flowers he came upon were western trillium. He leaned down and fingered the leaves, the last few wilted flowers, once white, now purple. He came next to a patch of hellebore. He saw it sidelong in the dimness. The woods grew darker. He squatted at several places on the path, but he had to guess at the flowers that came under his searching hands.

At a clearing there was more light. He recognized purslane and wood sorrel. He lay on the ground to bring his face close to the soil and inhaled the cold, damp perfume flowing there. He felt the prickers of trailing blackberry against his wrist. His delicate fingers found the pendulous flowers of wild bleeding heart. He recalled the first time he saw spotted cor-alroot, the first time he smelled deer-head orchid.

He lay in the clearing until he was stiff from the night air, then got up and walked back to the house. He returned the unused flashlight to the drawer, stood reading some pages in Haskin's book, then put out the light and went upstairs. He was in bed some minutes before his wife spoke.

"Do you know what she found today?" asked Alice.

"What's that?"

"*Eburophyton austinae.* She took me. I'd never seen one before."

Wick Colter recalled the page in Haskin exactly, the paragraph on the phantom orchid he had memorized as a boy: "It is truly a phantom, for which you may seek for years, and then, when least expected it suddenly stands before you in some dim forest aisle, a vision of soft, white loveliness, that once seen can never be forgotten."

"Me either," he said.

He felt the straight edge of his wife's hand against his thigh. "You only have to ask her."

"Yes," he answered, "though it might easily come to more than that if I'm to get home."

Was it night alone, sitting the open windowsill, he wondered.

"You smell like the woods," she said.

SONORA

Near the head of Golfo de California, on the Sonoran coast south of Cabo Tepoca, El Gran Desierto tapers tenuously to an end and a more nondescript country of dry barrancas and occasional water begins. It was along this desolate stretch of coastline that the Mexican philanthropist and businessman Ochetó de Mismas built his retreat of twelve thousand acres, with a comfortable house in the mission style, to which he flew ten or twelve times a year for a few days of relaxation and to swim in the gulf.

Among his many interests de Mismas was drawn to the physical sciences, and he sometimes attended international meetings to hear papers presented. At a meeting in Mexico City in 1988, of scientists and engineers working with difficult mathematical descriptions of turbulence in fluids, de Mismas was struck by the presentation of a young Canadian, a deaf man named Glenn Wycliff who had begun his career as a private student of Ralph Bagnold, the great English theoretician of the dynamics of wind-blown sand. In his paper, "The Double Curved Surface of Barchan Dunes at al-Kharijah," Wycliff described dunes near a line of oases in southern Egypt in language that, for a scientific presentation, was almost recklessly sensual. He made his colleagues as wary as he had made his famous mentor; but de Mismas found Wycliff's allusions provocative and stimulating. He invited him out to dinner. Over dessert, de Mismas made Wycliff an offer that took the young scientist by surprise. At his coastal home in Sonora, said de Mismas, there was an isolated colony of dunes. He was no expert, he insisted, but these dunes seemed an odd cross between coastal dunes and the draa, seif, and barchan dunes of interior deserts. Would Wycliff be interested in studying them, their shape and behavior? De Mismas would offer his home as a residence, plus a stipend and telephone and fax services. He would have a man come down every ten days or so from Puerto de Lobos, to the north, with fresh food. Wycliff was overwhelmed, and accepted. The two men embraced.

Even with a hearing aid in each ear, Wycliff could barely hear. He suffered from a deterioration of his auditory nerves, an irreversible condition but one that so far had compromised his work very little. His single regret was that it was not the esoteric evidence that sand dunes offered of the wind's sweep and caress that had originally drawn him to their study, but the sound dunes made, a somewhat prolonged, vibrant booming that issued from them, as if from church bells buried beneath. The phenomenon was little studied, its cause unknown. Recordings Wycliff once heard had astonished and then haunted him; but the gradual loss of his hearing had pointed him in another direction, into the study of the types of curves winds create in dune fields and on the surface of dune seas. The de Mismas dunes would provide him an opportunity to study a system that was geographically isolated and, as de Mismas described it, unaffected either by the growth of vegetation or by the meanders of domestic stock.

Wycliff told de Mismas he had to finish a year of teaching, a temporary position at the University of

Leeds, but that he would be able to move out to de Mismas's estancia in Sonora in a few months. De Mismas said he would be glad to support him for several years, that Wycliff should bring a companion if he wished, and that he, de Mismas, would be visiting, but not frequently. Perhaps during such times, de Mismas suggested, Wycliff might want to go off for a few days to explore. Wycliff agreed enthusiastically with all of this, but on the flight back to Leeds he became troubled by what in de Mismas's presence had seemed so suitable. He could not think of a companion—a woman—to go with him; and he did not entirely relish the idea of so many months alone. As his hearing failed, so, too, had his circle of friends diminished. His hearing might finally wane completely while he was living at de Mismas's; he wondered if under those circumstances he might develop the flat, toneless voice of the profoundly deaf, yet not know it. He might, then, lose what little sociability he had left.

These thoughts did not stay with him long, however. He was buoyed by feelings of anticipation for the work, had strong feelings of gratitude toward de Mismas, a sense of personal fortune, and a nearly physical desire for the sublime beauty of the dunes, emotions that all ran together with him.

. . .

Wycliff arrived at the de Mismas house in August, a single passenger, with Hector Gutierrez, de Mismas's pilot. It took him some weeks to accustom himself to the heat, but by October he had in place a regular schedule of work and a grasp of his research problems. The dunes were more attractive, both mathematically and aesthetically, than de Mismas had been able to make clear. They stood inland from the sea about a mile and were nearly two square miles in extent, rising to a height of sixty or seventy feet. They were surrounded on three sides by a vast playa and on the west by a scabrous plain with little vegetation. Within this space, like dancers on a stage, the dunes shifted continuously, year after year, an enormously complex movement that left some dunes isolated for months at the periphery or in the interior of the dune field before they were reincorporated. All this Wycliff deduced by hiking around and through the dunes and from the first few months of data from his recording anemometers.

De Mismas visited twice in the fall with Gutierrez, both times insisting Wycliff not disturb his research by going away. De Mismas listened attentively to Wycliff's description of his work and walked across the dunes with him on each occasion. Wycliff, comparing the first meeting with a less-than-enthusiastic second meeting, and contrasting in his mind the different ways de Mismas had paid attention, worried that he had become long-winded and boring on the subject of wind-shaped dunes, that de Mismas might be having some second thoughts about his generosity. Just before Christmas, de Mismas faxed to ask Wycliff if he might take a short trip, as they had once agreed, so that de Mismas might have the house alone at Christmas time. Wycliff made every effort to be gracious in assenting, but he felt turned out.

De Mismas maintained this arrangement into the spring, telling Wycliff each time he wanted to come up from Mexico City that he would like the house to himself. Wycliff was hurt. His hearing was so diminished now he could hardly detect sound. His isolation, his truncation, felt extreme. He longed, too, for a woman's company, sometimes to the point of anguish. This desire was exacerbated by wandering the sensuous forms of the dunes, his body, like the dunes, tongued by breezes from the sea or by hot winds from the interior. But he did not hold on to these depressions. The research he was doing, measuring the changing radius of curvature of a single dune, correlating this to a pattern of seasonal winds and observing changes in the heights of individual dunes (as though the dune field were breathing through a year, inhaling and exhaling)—all this complexity held his imagination and soothed him.

One day in June a fax arrived saying Ochetó de Mismas was coming up with two friends, that he would welcome Wycliff's company, and that Wycliff should plan to stay at the house, to take his meals with them and perhaps enjoy a swim together.

Wycliff did not sense the plane's approach. He was intently photographing a ridge, a place where two dunes that had once merged were again separating, when he saw the Cessna's shadow cross in the frame. He looked up to see the blue and white plane wagging its wings and starting its downwind turn. He collected his notebook and equipment and walked back to his Honda three-wheeler.

Wycliff pulled up at the airstrip with a luggage trailer just as Hector was shutting the engines down. Hector signaled from the pilot's seat, *hola*. Wycliff could see de Mismas exiting onto the wing on the far side to assist his passengers, and he brought the trailer around. He had expected, for some reason, two of de Mismas's business associates—there was nothing in the house to suggest de Mismas ever came with his family—but these were two young women. They were dressed expensively and fashionably, as was de Mismas, as though all of them had just come from a party. De Mismas was, as usual, impeccably groomed. He remembered de Mismas's cultured voice, the deep, lilting run of his language, how perfectly it matched the gracious movements he saw now as de Mismas helped the women in high heels down the plane's two-step ladder. They all wore impenetrable dark glasses. One of the women wore a white silk dress. In the brilliant light Wycliff could see the shadow of her slip, and, when wind pressed around the airplane, the outline of her nipples and the interior curve of her thighs. In spite of the heat and the confinement of the plane, both women seemed fresh—poised and energetic. Wycliff initially took them for models. He expected them to move with languid boredom. But then he realized their breasts were too large and they seemed, to him, too ebullient to be models. As quickly, he realized they were an expression of de Mismas's appetite, that they were here for him.

De Mismas introduced him to Estrella, with a mane of blue-black hair, and to Mora, in the white dress, and asked if he would help Hector. The women smiled at him, shook hands in a friendly way, and began walking toward the house with de Mismas, arm in arm.

Hector had already started loading the trailer with

soft leather baggage and insulated food containers. Wycliff could speech-read Spanish, but Hector, in an effort to help, would make it more difficult by exaggerating the movement of his lips and the other muscles of his face. Wycliff learned they had brought roast duck, veal, and salmon. Hector would heat it all in the microwave and prepare the vegetables and salads fresh. Hector swept his hand over the containers and made an exaggerated, conspiratorial face, as though to eat like this was to get away with something.

"Las chicas?" inquired Wycliff.

Hector, crossing his legs and pulling his fists repeatedly toward his belly, made an extreme gesture of pain and joy. Then he shook his right hand violently, as though he had burned it.

Wycliff wanted to ask if Hector knew why de Mismas had asked him to stay, but he decided the question would reveal an intention he did not have. Hector had pulled a broomstick from the luggage compartment and stepped to the edge of the airstrip, where he began tossing small stones in the air and slamming them off into the desert with terrific swings. Wycliff was aware of the sharply rising whir of the stick, like a quail exploding from brush, and of the click and whine of the stone as it cut the desert air. But he heard neither.

. . .

De Mismas settled the women in a single bedroom that looked out onto the gulf and which communicated with his own bedroom. De Mismas had decorated the house with pieces of Aztec and Mayan pottery and with works by contemporary Mexican sculptors and painters. Wycliff had put the rooms in perfect order that morning, and the women, to whom de Mismas was giving a tour, were complimenting de Mismas on his taste and on the design of his home when Hector and Wycliff walked in with the luggage.

"My young friend," began de Mismas in Spanish, gesturing toward Wycliff, "is an eminent scientist, a man with an international standing, but he keeps a beautiful house." They all laughed except Wycliff, who merely smiled and nodded. Mora held his eyes for a fraction longer than he expected, and he looked away, acutely conscious of her physical presence and of a physical longing that arose in him, which felt wild and dangerous under the circumstances.

"Why don't we change," said de Mismas in English, "then you can tell us, Glenn, what you have been doing. I'm sure the ladies would appreciate it."

Wycliff helped Hector prepare a lunch of fresh fruit and cold salmon. When he met Hector's eye, Hector read his mind and made a long, painful face, cupping his crotch with one hand. Wycliff realized in that moment that his own physical desire had overwhelmed another longing, a hope as desperate, as intense, for another sort of union.

They ate lunch in a mirador, a gazebo separate from the house, where the wind off the water cooled them. Wycliff explained his research at de Mismas's gentle urging, though he felt it was too esoteric a subject, too great a presumption on his part. The women listened attentively and, to his surprise, asked questions that seemed more than polite. He was restrained in his responses, for fear of losing their attention. Again, Mora gave him to believe, with a direct look and turn of her smile, that she understood and appreciated what he was saying. And that she liked him.

"Let's swim, shall we?" announced de Mismas, rising from the table. He nodded to Hector to clear the dishes, motioned the women to their room with a dismissive movement of his hand, and then said, "Will you take a swim, Glenn?"

"Yes, sure," said Wycliff.

"Do you like them?"

"The women?"

"Yes, Glenn. Is there someone else here?"

"Well they seem very . . . spirited. Very nice women. Bright, good-looking."

De Mismas gazed out over the gulf with the air of a magnate. "Do you want to take one?"

"Want?"

"Yes! Why else are they here? If you wish, they will listen politely all night while you discuss complicated theoretical approaches to the study of turbulence—and, I can tell you, they will love your descriptions of dunes when you get into that ecstatic state of yours—but they are here, really, for us to fuck. Do you want to sleep with Mora?"

Wycliff could not respond, though his mouth moved in the shape of words.

"These are clean women," offered de Mismas. "There is no problem with that. Is there a difficulty I do not see? Is it men?"

"No," Wycliff blurted.

"Can you understand them, then? Their English is not very good."

"No, I can read them . . . Mora more easily."

"Go, change. Later, if you decide you want Mora, just take her to bed. I give you that. I am not offended. I respect you. I respect what you are doing, and realize you are lonely out here."

He had not been in the water for more than a week. He enjoyed thinking of himself as a mote in the great gulf, suspended just there where its waves washed up on the Mexican shore, their energy dissipating into heat and increasing the Earth's spin to a degree too slight to measure. Mora swam toward him. On the beach he had been embarrassed by the urge to look at her, at her taut, voluptuous body, the delicate bones of her face, at the utterly unblemished skin. Her green eyes.

"What is it for you?" she asked, treading water next to him.

"What?"

"You understand my lips?" she said.

"Yes, sí."

"You want a friend?"

"Yes. I have been here many months by myself!"

"That is too bad. I can fix that, you know?"

"Is that true?"

"Yes. The choice, all my life, I make that."

She swam off, with a look that transfixed him. He continued treading water with smooth, coordinated movements of his limbs, like a salmon at the edge of a rapid.

Hector prepared veal for dinner and a large green salad. Afterward, de Mismas showed slides of two trips he had made recently, one to Athens and the second to a part of the Namib Desert Wycliff himself had always wanted to visit, huge dune fields around Sossusvlei, west of Sesriem and the Naukluft Mountains.

"Glenn, you would have appreciated this country," said de Mismas urbanely. "But didn't you, you told me, earlier in your career, travel to Tanzania to see some dunes of volcanic ash? And weren't you also in northern Algeria, studying gypsum dunes?"

"You have a very good memory, Señor de Mismas." De Mismas had been like this all evening, giving him an opportunity to participate more fully in the conversation, even to embroider his accomplishments. He wanted to trust de Mismas, but he sensed the edge of something. He remained deferential and did not exaggerate his stories.

They finished the evening in the mirador, sipping aquavit, the four of them, Hector having gone to bed. The women wore shawls. De Mismas speculated about Mexico's economic future and spoke about Mexican politics in a way that was very engaging, with philosophical acceptance and humor.

"Shall we go in, Estrella?" he said finally.

Wycliff's sexual desire surged as they departed, but it was tempered now by other emotions. He appreciated the suggestion of depth in Mora's company. He felt much more at ease than he had earlier in the day. When Estrella and de Mismas left, Mora leaned over and blew out the two large candles on the table, which had been guttering in the wind.

"I can't understand you if I can't see your face," said Wycliff.

Mora waved her hand in front of him. Who wishes to talk? Our warmth, our attentiveness to each other, this will not be enough?

They were on a wrought-iron bench. When he reached an arm around her she moved closer to rest against him. They gazed at the starlit gulf. After a time, Mora pressed him gently.

Rising suddenly to his feet he felt dizzy and, with his first steps, a flood of anxiety. What had started hours before as driven, sexual desire was now a desire, nearly painful, for companionship. He knew that this arrangement, sleeping with her, de Mismas's involvement with each of them, would not help. He followed close behind on the path to the house, breathing her. His desire, when he tested it like a man nervously twanging a bowstring, was intense. He had been here before; the sex would not be enough. He craved what was unbounded, impossible. He wanted to move with her beneath the surface of their bodies.

They stepped through the sliding doors into the living room to see Estrella and de Mismas stretched out together on the couch watching the large-screen television.

"*Treasure of the Sierra Madre*, en Español," said de Mismas. "Have you read him, Glenn: Traven?"

He shook his head. He could hardly see de Mismas's words in the soft blue light.

"We are to bed now," said Mora. She tugged lightly on his arm. They all said good night. He followed her to his room at the opposite end of the house. She looked around, then turned the light on in his bathroom.

"Can you shower while I come back?" she asked. She looked at him with unexpected sweetness.

He showered. She returned wearing her high heels and a powder blue peignoir. He sat naked at the edge of the bed looking at the large, dark aureoles of her breasts. She cradled his head against her stomach. He slid back, turning the sheets, reaching for her hand. She stepped out of her shoes, crossed over him nimbly, and stretched out with her hands overlapped on his hip. The intensity of her desire, the hunger he sensed in her touch, frightened him. He wondered if making love would make the loneliness disappear or only deepen it. The moment, he felt, was precarious for him.

"When the moon is full," he said, "and I wake up before dawn, I go out to the dunes. Sometimes there is dew on the sand. It twinkles—do you know that word?—twinkles in the moonlight, like stars. The dunes look like a cluster of stars then, a galaxy, stretching away to the Sierra de San Antonio. It's like standing outside the universe, looking back.

"Do you ever think about things like that?" he asked her.

She moved her head gently, no, against his chest.

"I think about them. More, even, maybe than about this," he said, lining her breast with his hand. He shifted, to pull her against him, to give her the hollow of his shoulder. He wanted to trust her company, to act on the genuineness of their passion, but he could not move.

He became aware after a while of her fingers, tapping softly on his chest. He lifted his head to look. She put a finger to her ear and then, her eyes wide, pointed to the ceiling. He did not understand. She tapped her temple, as though urging him to listen, and then made an abrupt, undulating motion with her hand, which he knew, unmistakably, was wind.

He went to the window. A storm had broken on the coast and was sweeping inland. With his hands pressed to the wall he could feel what he was not able to hear.

Mora, naked, had pulled on one of his T-shirts.

When their eyes met she made a smooth gesture with her hand, indicating they should go out. He began searching for his pants, wondering what he had for her to wear.

She was still looking straight at him. "You, either, are not owned," she said, lifting her chin to him and smiling.

The big winds would wobble them, he thought, until they reached the dunes. Then warm, still air would envelop them, and the deep current of the wind would roar over whatever hollow in the dunes they chose.

LESSONS

FROM

THE

WOLVERINE

*I*n the Ruby Mountains, where the Sanumavik River heads, there is supposed to be living now, and for as far back as memory can go, a family of wolverine. I first learned about them in an offhand way, so often the case with information like this, which turns up in a remote village and subsequently proves startling or strange.

One evening I was playing catch with a boy named Narvalaq, a boy of twelve in a village on the Koanik River, part of the Sanumavik drainage. I missed a throw and had to retrieve the ball from the river. It landed in shallow water trickling over a point bar, beautiful cobbles—reds, grays, greens, browns. Walking back, I moved slowly, stooped over, studying rocks that had been polished by the river and now were shining in the late evening light, each one bright as an animal's eye.

Narvalaq came up and said, "Wolverine, up at Caribou Caught by the Head Creek, they walk along like that. That's how you know it's them."

I nodded. I wanted to think it over, but right away I was interested in what he had to say. First I believed he meant that wolverine living at that place looked very closely at stones or at other things in the river, that they studied things more than other wolverines do. But I learned later in a conversation with Elisha Atnah, Narvalaq's father, that they just like to walk in the shallows. When these Caribou-Caught-by-the-Head wolverine are traveling alongside water they like to walk in it.

"Like you did that time," said Elisha.

The village where I was told this is called Eedaqna. A year after it happened I got back to Eedaqna—but perhaps I should tell you a little about myself first, so you will understand more about this story. I grew up in the West Indies, Antigua, around there. We lost my mother in a hurricane, big flood.

In 1974, when I was eight, we moved to Tennessee, my father and I. He taught mathematics at Union University. I began walking in the hills then, looking at animals. I liked being near them. In 1978 my father died and I went to northern Alberta to live with his brother. I tried to get the knack of going to school when I lived there, but I couldn't. I liked to walk around on the prairie, along the creeks. One thing I did then was to fly falcons. I liked being out with them, watching them circle overhead, getting a sense of the country I couldn't get. But it was hard keeping them in cages. I couldn't keep it up.

I ended up working on prop planes in Edmonton when I was eighteen, which I got very good at. I've had good jobs all along. Every time I left one—Peace River, Fort Smith, Yellowknife—I went farther north. In 1989 I moved to Kaktovik, where I still am. I haven't started a family yet, which is all right with me, but my friends in the coastal villages and up in the Brooks Range don't like it. They don't talk to me quite as much because I don't have a family. No children. They believe it's strange. But they have strangeness in their own lives.

I didn't forget what Narvalaq said. I thought it was something to know, what he had said about the wolverine. So the first time I could I went back to Eedaqna, when a Cessna 206 crashed there. Maybe someone would tell me something more. I talked to an old man working with me on the plane, Abraham Roosevelt, trying to move the conversation around to wolverines up on the Sanumavik. (I don't know another way with them except backing into it.) First, I said I might move to Eedaqna. Maybe, he said. I said I might trap in the winter, then go north to Kaktovik in summer to work on planes. He said maybe I would do that. Then I said if I trapped, I'd want to trap where no one else was, even if I had to travel a long way every day to my trapline. He said that might be good. Where would I go? I asked. Lots of places to go, he said. What about the Ruby Mountains, I said, up there at the head of the Sanu-mavik, was that too far? That's not a good place, he said, not too good. Why? He looked at me for a moment then went back to work on one of the carbu-retors. He talked about one family that had lost a lot when this plane went down. Everyone was trying to help them now. Later, he said to me, "Wolverine that live up that way, Sanumavik River, they don't like it when people trap. They don't have that up there."

That conversation, when I first learned how those wolverine felt, happened in the spring of 1990. The following winter I met a woman named Dora Kahvi-nook living in Kaktovik, but who was from Eedaqna.

She took a liking to me, and I liked her, too. She told me some stories that were unusual for her to have, hunting stories about her two brothers and her father. I asked if her father or her brothers had ever gone hunting in the upper Sanumavik. She said no. I said two people in Eedaqna had told me that the wolverine that lived up there didn't like people coming up. She said she didn't know, but, yes, that's what people said.

That winter I dreamed four times about wolverine. I decided I was going to go up there when spring came, regardless. I've never been able to learn what I want to know about animals from books or looking at television. I have to walk around near them, be in places where they are. This was the heart of the trouble that I had in school. Many of the stories that should have been told about animals, about how they live, their different ways, were never told. I don't know what the stories were, but when I walked in the woods or out on the prairie or in the mountains, I could feel the boundaries of those stories. I knew they were there, the way you know fish are in a river. This knowledge was what I wanted, and the only way I had gotten it was to go out and look for it. To be near animals until they showed you something that you didn't imagine or you hadn't seen or heard.

In June I went back to Eedaqna and asked Elisha

Atnah if he would travel with me. I told him I had
felt the wolverine up on the Sanumavik River pulling
on me over the winter. They didn't leave me alone.
He listened and a few days later he said he would
go with me. We traveled down the Koanik and then
up the Sanumavik. It was a long way and we walked,
we didn't take three-wheelers. Elisha said it would
be better to walk. We walked for three days. In the
evening, I asked Elisha questions.

"How many families of wolverine live up there?"

"Just that one. But it's a big family, they have
been up there as long as anyone remembers. That's
all their country."

"Are they different from other wolverine, like ones
living over on Sadlerochit?"

"Wolverines are all different. Each family, different."

After a while he came back to this. He said,
"Wolverines have culture, same as people do, but
they all look the same to some people because they
carry it in their heads. That's how all animals are
different. Almost all their culture—I think that's the
word I mean—it's inside their heads."

"You mean tools, drums, winter clothing—things
like that?"

"That's right. Everything they need—stories,
which way to travel, a way to understand the world—

that's all in their heads. Sometimes you will find a bed they have made, or a little house, or maybe where they have made marks on the ground for dancing. You might sometime see a fox riding a piece of wood down a river where he is going. But you don't see many things like that. Their winter clothes—they just come out from inside them."

"Which story is the one that tells a person not to set a trapline in this country we are going to?"

"One time, long time ago, before my father can remember, we trapped in that country. Some marten and lynx. River otter. Mink and short-tailed weasel. For some reason, no one trapped wolves there. We left wolves alone but we looked really hard for wolverine. My father's uncle, Tusamik, he belonged to that place then, and his youngest boy, he started setting every kind of trap along one creek. Moon Hiding the Daylight Creek. He found a caribou there, pretty much finished up, and he set traps around it. He didn't come back until five days later, maybe—too many days. He didn't understand, that country was very generous to us. He had caught a wolverine, one front foot, one back foot." Here, Elisha stood up and showed me how the wolverine was stretched out. "But the wolverine, she was standing on top of a wolf! She had gotten the life out of him. Killed him. And there was also blood from another wolf in the snow. Tusamik's boy studied what had happened, each animal's marks. The wolverine had first been caught by a front foot. Then the two wolves had come along. That caribou meat was there, but for some reason they wanted the life in that wolverine, so they tried to get it. They came at her at the same time from two directions. The wolverine, she killed the first wolf right away—and all the time she was jumping around with that trap on her foot. Then she stepped in the second trap, with her back foot, and she couldn't move very much. But she had hurt that other wolf already. It went away. The boy thought it all happened two days, maybe, before he got there.

"The wolverine was angry. She told the boy it was over, wolverines were not going to do this anymore. The boy said he was sorry, but the wolverine said no, there won't be any more trapping for a while. Too many days waiting for him.

"So, we don't trap any animals there now. We don't go up there too much."

We went away from the Sanumavik River the next day, up Caribou Caught by the Head Creek. When we got to a place where the tundra was hilly and open, only a few trees, willows, around, Elisha said he was going to leave. He told me to just sit there and wait. In the afternoon I saw two wolverine at the crest of a hill. They came down close to the creek where I was and lay down in the sunshine on the far side and went to sleep. I had backed up against some rocks that were warm from the sun and I went to sleep, too. I began dreaming about the wolverines. It was night. I saw the two of them lying on their backs on the side of the hill. They were talking. They motioned for me to come over and lie down next to them. I did. It was dark all over the tundra. They were talking about the stars.

"You have to pay attention," one of them said. "We're going to show you something."

I looked up into the sky and along one edge of the Milky Way I could see it was different. The stars were quivering in a pattern along that edge. It was like water running over a shallows in the sunshine.

"Look in there," said the other wolverine. "Look right in there."

I looked into the pattern. I was a bird then, looking down like an osprey, flying high over the water, a river moving across the tundra. I could see many things moving in the current. Fish. Under the water I saw shells, sand, the colors of Antigua. Then leaves turning in the current, like they did in the Hatchie in Tennessee in the fall. One leaf was my father's face. Other people. Then the face of a wild dog, a crazy animal, sick. I remember my father fighting in the woods with that dog. Then for a long time leaves—the faces of animals I had seen in the woods in Tennessee and away in Alberta. The leaves were many colors and shapes. Tulip trees and poplars. Some faces, some animals, I remembered. I felt sad and tried to pull my eyes away but I couldn't. I started to remember them all, every one of those animals.

"I'm afraid," I said. "I want to get down, come down to the ground now." But nothing happened.

"Keep going," said one of the wolverines.

Looking upriver, the water was green. Looking the other way, downriver, it was bluer. Below me it was all transparent. Leaves tumbling there. The river spilled over a line of black mountains far away, through a dark blue sky. A wind was blowing and I was cold. I wanted to get down. Then I saw myself below, looking up, shading my eyes with the heavy glove, the jesses in my other hand. I was waving.

"This is our power," said one of the wolverines.

Where I was looking, in still water, the faces were trembling like aspen leaves in a wind. Animals I recognized—black bear, snapping turtle, lark sparrow, monarch butterfly, corn snake, wolf spider, porcupine, yellow-shafted flicker, muskellunge— memories of those days. Trembling like leaves on a branch. A curtain of willow leaves, through which sunlight blinked. I heard my heart beat, regular, loud. I lay on the ground, my back sideways against warm rocks. I was looking out through river willows at a hillside. The wolverines weren't there anymore.

I sat up and looked around for Elisha. He wasn't there either. I waded the creek. Where the wolverine had been the grass was pressed down but there were no tracks. I stood there for a long time, watching the sky, the hills, all around.

From where I stood I could see across to where Elisha had left me, by rocks that were dotted with bright orange and yellow lichen. On one of the rocks I could see something. I crossed back over and walked up to it. It was a willow stick, about two feet long and curved like a small bow. It had been carved to look like a wolverine running, raising its back in that strange way they have when they are hurrying along. Tied around the neck was a string of ten wolverine claws. It looked too strong to pick up. I left it on the rock and sat down to wait for Elisha.

After a while I picked up the wolverine stick and held it in my lap. Elisha came from a direction I wasn't looking, from the Sanumavik River. We went back there and camped. He said the claws were from the left front foot and the right rear foot of a wolverine. Female, he said. I told him about seeing the animals from my past. I felt them all around. I felt I was carrying something in my head that hadn't been there before. He said he was glad.

Elisha said he didn't know what the stick animal meant. He told me to carry it, not to put it inside my pack. He said we could ask someone when we got back to Eedaqna.

THE

RUNNER

My sister and I have not gotten on well for a long time. When we were younger it was a matter of politics, her abandonment of her religion, her choice of male companions—on two occasions choices that left her destitute. She is older by two years but somehow in our twenties I began thinking of her as younger. Now, as I turn thirty-seven, I have to remind myself that *I'm* younger.

A difficult thing I'm having to face is that after many years of condescension I've begun to feel admiration for her. It's even harder for me to admit after all these years of criticism that what's driving me to maintain contact with her is a desire to know her. I want to try to fill a gaping hole, full of anger and regret, that's just visible to me now.

You can picture, perhaps, the unremarkable issues that separated us. I'm embarrassed at how predictable I've been, understanding how little she's changed during these years. I left behind a politics founded in naïveté, on impractical solutions to intractable problems, while she continued to embrace a politics of ideals. She believed—despite the evidence of history, which shows humans are selfish and aggrandizing. As for marriage, which she quickly came to see as not an arrangement for her, I'll not lie and claim I was honorable, if love and honor are interchangeable in a marriage. I married someone I loved, but I would not have loved her had she not been practical and devoted, had she not wanted to have children and help me finish law school. We're divorced now. When I look back on our history together, it seems inevitable. Perhaps one day this rapprochement I want with Mirara will seem the same.

An area of difficulty I suspect Mirara and I won't easily work out is religion. We were raised Catholic.

I'm still a practicing Catholic, as they say, but the divorce and certain issues like the Church's opposition to social reform in Latin America have made me less enthusiastic. Still, I believe the Church is brave, and correct, on other matters—abortion, for example, and in its reluctance to embrace homosexuality (despite Christ's example of Love). I don't think Mirara's ever had an abortion, but nothing puts us off each other like this does. She has no religion, just her friends and her solitary hiking and running, a life that has its attraction but in which all moral issues are murky, undefined by any laws.

Here, perhaps, is our crucial difference. I have always believed in abiding by the law (whether or not I actually did), where Mirara has been indifferent to most law. She's not been lawless, of course, not criminal; but she has a way of carrying herself above the law I find not only tiresome but anarchic, a destructive seed. I believe this.

The door that's opened between Mirara and me was opened by an unlikely person, a client, a man with substantial real estate holdings in Phoenix but an entertaining investor in many odder things as well. At our regular breakfast meeting he handed me a clipping from the Flagstaff paper, a story about a woman who'd found three large Anasazi storage jars at an undisclosed location in Grand Canyon National Park. According to the story, the polychrome jars, in perfect condition and nearly three feet tall, had become part of a new visitor display at the canyon. The woman, the story went on, had found them while climbing below the North Rim several years before.

I knew the woman was my sister as I read the piece, as surely as I intuited why Hamilton had given it to me.

"What do you think?" he asked. "We get some of those gung ho kids up at Northern Arizona or Prescott to do this for us. Pay them a salary, underwrite the cost of the trips—I'm talking outside the park, of course—in exchange for whatever they come up with. With adequate compensation. Here's my thought. Most of the Southwest has been scoured by pothunters. The easy places are done. The last stuff is in places like this, places nobody can get to, except these athletic kids with their high-tech rock-climbing gear. We send them around to these canyons on the Colorado Plateau, tell them to climb up to every cave opening they see—do you see this? What we acquire we sell or hold or even donate—whatever seems good."

"If you were the Park Service, Ham, or maybe the Heard Museum, you might get kids like them to do this. But for you, no way. They're too antibusiness, too idealistic."

"So we set up a foundation. What about the law on this? Can you keep what you find on public land, as long as it's not a national park or something? What if we just worked with private landholders, we'd be legitimate all the way. These kids would get into it, Steve. Preservation, Indians. They live for this kind of stuff. *I* can identify with it—great adventure, physical risk, financial reward. Look at pro athletes, for Chrissakes."

"I'll research the applicable law. There's federal law, Arizona's got laws. I don't think this is for you."

"Fair enough. We'll talk later. Here's another one," he said. He handed me a clipping from the Bisbee paper, about antique tinware.

When I got back to the office I Xeroxed the story about the Anasazi jars, wrote "Is this you?" across the top and sent it to Mirara in Winslow. Three days later I got it back with an exclamation mark after my question. The same evening I phoned her. We talked about the jars, we tried to talk about other things— her job with the city manager; our parents, retired but still living in Michigan; even our rival alma maters' football game that year (Notre Dame 38, Michigan 17)—but none of this went anywhere.

For a reason I can't explain—and at the time thought might be an overreaction—I drove up to Grand Canyon that weekend to look at the jars. They were lovely. I read the typescript handout, reporting what Mirara had already told me—the pots had been found in a small cave in a sheer wall, 150 feet above the canyon floor. But what was Mirara's arrangement with the Park Service? A ranger at the exhibit, a woman, was adamant—no answers, even when I told her I was Mirara's brother. She told me to speak with the park archeologist. After an awkward moment when I had to admit I knew very little about what my sister did, this fellow told me Mirara was "just a friend to the park," and that she'd found other things in the canyon over the years—twisted willow-twig figures, clay jars, even pieces of bark clothing.

"Mirara's more knowledgeable than anyone, I think," he offered, "about trails in the canyon. She was the first to find routes down to the river through Specter and Matkatamiba, on the South Rim. I know she's pioneered two or three routes off the North Rim. You should talk to her about it."

I ignored his jibe. Specter and Matkatamiba were side canyons, I supposed.

"Do you have her address?" he said. "I'm afraid her phone's not listed."

Jesus, I thought. "Yes, I've got her address. We're

in touch regularly, it's just that I don't know much about this part of her life."

"Well, it's a hell of a lot more important to her than her job, I can tell you that."

"Well thank you. I'm glad to know that. I think I'll give her a call and take her out to dinner in Flagstaff. You've been very helpful. Thank you."

I did call. She said she'd be happy to fix a late dinner if I'd make the drive out from Flagstaff.

On the way there I thought more about the canyon than I did about Mirara. Our parents had brought us there when we were kids, in 1968. Mirara went back every year after that. I made one trip with the Boy Scouts. We hiked down Bright Angel Trail to Phantom Ranch and then rode rafts down the Colorado River through Unkar and Hance and Sockdolager rapids. Thinking about it made me remorseful. For all I gained on that trip, I never went back. Carol and I went up two or three times with the kids. Carol wanted to buy a house up there and Geoffrey and Lisa loved going but I just couldn't get interested in it. It seemed like a place you went when you were a kid, then you took your kids to it.

Maybe I could do it again, hike down the trail, raft the river through the big rapids. When I looked out over the canyon that day, after I called Mirara, it seemed welcoming.

Mirara, it turned out, had two broken ribs, which is why she didn't want to drive over to meet me in Flagstaff. And she had a guest, a young man named Ned Wearny, a student at Prescott. I resented his being there. He was far too young for my sister— what now? I thought as we shook hands—and he made it impossible for me to speak openly. As dinner proceeded, however, Ned grew on me, with his earnestness and his stories about climbing in Nepal and studying drumming somewhere in Africa. He was a very serious and determined young man. I couldn't get the reason he was with my sister, but Mirara had not had good luck with men, so maybe this was a new direction. I asked her once when she was going to get married. "I'm very happy," she told me. "That doesn't mean I'll never get married. But I'm not staring at the horizon."

She'd broken her ribs in a fall in the canyon the week before. I wanted to learn more about her hiking and climbing, but I didn't feel comfortable exposing the rift between us in front of young Ned, so I pretended to know more than I did, which meant I learned more about Ned than I did about what my sister was doing.

After dinner I had to leave. I wanted to get back to Phoenix even if it was very late, so I could get a fresh start in the office in the morning. Ned wanted to know if I'd give him a lift to Flagstaff. He had friends there. By all means, I said. I told Mirara I'd call her the next night. I'd been charmed, actually, by the way she carried herself. She had mannerisms, ways of moving her hands, a slang diction that she'd acquired over the years, that irked me; but she guided the conversation so Ned could talk about himself and she didn't insist that I listen to any music, which she used to do.

"So where did you meet Mirara," I asked Ned when we got out on the Interstate.

"Well, I heard about her, like everybody else, you know, but, actually, I met her first when I was hiking in the canyon, going solo over the Nankoweap."

"Nankoweap Trail?"

"Yeah, over on the North Rim. There's a lot of exposure on that trail. It's only about four inches wide in some places, really dangerous scree. No water. I met her in a place where it was pretty easy to get by. We said hello. The thing was, she was running, you know, so I didn't want to stop her to talk. But I knew right away it was Mirara Graham."

"She was running down the trail?"

"No. Up. It was September, you know, overcast day. Cool. She ran with these two water bottles in her fists. As far as I know she'd already been to the end of the trail and was coming out, which meant she must have started in the dark, way before sunrise, which is pretty scary."

"Yeah."

"But, that's your sister, man."

"Tell me something—I don't want to pry—but, are you and Mirara . . . ah . . ."

He looked at me blankly. No help.

"Are you together?"

"You mean, like, are we seeing each other?"

"Yes."

"No, no. I go over there to talk to her once in a while, talk about the trails you know. Mirara has spent maybe eight hundred days below the rim. She's covered every trail known in the canyon and discovered about ten. Plus, she's climbed all over down there. That's how she found those jars. She's done *that* about ten times, too, I guess. She spots a place, just goes to it. Over the years, you know, the canyon's changed. Some of the miners' trails from the eighties and nineties, big enough to move ore across, they're gone now. Collapsed. Most of the really old trails, the Anasazi trails, are gone, too. Rock slides, erosion. So you see these isolated caves with no trails to them, just sheer cliff faces. So she's found a bunch of those and climbed up to them."

"Is there very often Anasazi pottery in them?"

"Sometimes. What you need to understand, though, is that, for her, it's not like she's looking for anything. She just walks and climbs and runs. And sometimes she finds things."

"So you talk to her about the trails?"

"Sure. But—well, a lot of us, five or six people I know, just like to talk with her. She's very satisfying to be around. She set out to do something, she's still doing it, and she doesn't want to do anything else. For somebody like me—I'm twenty and still don't know what I want to do—she's good to be with. She's more gentle, more focused, than anyone I know."

"Do you hike or run with her?"

"See, that's the thing. You'd like to. But she asks you only once in a great while. And, brother, if you're called, you better be ready."

"Have you gone with her?"

"Twice. Once down the Atwater, off the North Rim in the west canyon, another time down the Enfilade Point Trail, also off the North Rim. Harvey Butchart pioneered the Enfilade around 1961 or so, but Mirara discovered the Atwater. The Park Service calls it the Atwater after some miner. She calls it something else. It was an Anasazi trail first."

"These were good trips?"

"They were scary, is what they were. I mean, you

155

have to be at a certain level to keep up with her. I don't mean just to keep up physically. It's psychological and spiritual. That Atwater trail, there's some radical exposure there—five hundred feet of Redwall below you, two hundred feet above you and you're on a trail that's no wider than your shoes. You have to take hold of yourself. That's the psychological part. The spiritual part—she makes you think about what you believe in when you're with her, because what she believes in you can see. It's in the way she moves. She runs all those long trails, you know, on the rim, the Widforss and the rest. You watch her, you'll see her stride, her hand balance, is perfectly matched to the ground. I mean perfect. It's beautiful."

"Do you—excuse me, this is all new—do people run for records on these trails, like quickest down and back?"

"Some people do that. I think Mirara is probably pretty quick, but quickness is not her thing. What she would do, for example, what I did with her on the Enfilade, was we would go along a ways and then go up a ravine, climb five hundred feet and maybe find some pictographs or petroglyphs. Or watch deer or bighorn sheep moving up the side of a bay. She'd study that so hard, you didn't have a prayer, right then, of getting a question answered. And I know, other times, she has gone to the bottom, drifted and swum across the river and come up another trail. In one day. Start in the dark, finish in the dark.

"You learn a lot when you're with her. She sees a lot of things you miss, but she never makes you feel stupid because you missed them. And you know when you're with her you're going to see something incredible, because she's given herself away to the place, and it's how it responds to her."

I wanted to tell Ned how we'd first come to the canyon in 1968, but couldn't find words that didn't sound like I was laying partial claim to something I knew nothing about.

"I heard a story about her one time—you hear lots of stories about Mirara, and she likes to hear them, too, because a lot of them aren't true, but this one is—about a time some people on a raft trip saw her running along the edge of the river. They passed her first just above Grapevine. Now, as far as I know, there's no trail around Grapevine, nothing, but when these people pulled over for lunch below the rapid they saw her again and she wasn't wet so they knew, the guides knew, she'd some way gotten around that. There she was, on the far bank, just running on down the river. They passed her again about an hour later.

She runs like a deer sometimes, way up on her toes with those long legs, you know, so you almost hold your breath watching her. The reason I think she goes into the canyon alone so often is that very few people, even really good free climbers, have that kind of balance. She has a hunger that's fed by moving through the canyon with that kind of balance."

I dropped Ned off at a bar in Flagstaff.

"Listen," he said after he got out, speaking through the passenger window, "if you want to read about this stuff, get hold of three books by Harvey Butchart. They're called *Grand Canyon Treks One, Two* and *Three*. They'll get you started. Butchart's from another time, but he's a trailblazer, you know. Get a feeling for it, then give Mirara a call. I bet you that'd make her happy."

"You know," I said, "I run in Phoenix. I did a 2:31 marathon this spring. I should get out on those trails. Maybe I'd meet Mirara, right?"

"Well, like I was saying, it's not so much that kind of running, for her."

"I know, I know. What I mean is, if I have the stamina, the physical stamina, then I might—then at least I might be ready for the rest. To try."

"That sure could happen." He tapped the door

frame lightly and nodded. "You take care, Mr. Graham," he said and walked away into the bar.

Ned's goodwill had a note of disbelief in it, which I carried all the way to Phoenix. By the time I got there, I wondered if it would ever be possible to reach my sister, if I could ever make up the ground.

A Note About the Author

Barry Lopez was born in Port Chester, New York, in 1945, grew up in southern California, attended prep school in New York City, and has lived in rural Oregon since 1968.

He is the author of *Arctic Dreams*, for which he received the National Book Award; *Of Wolves and Men*; several collections of stories and essays, including *Winter Count*, *River Notes*, and *Crossing Open Ground*; and *Crow and Weasel*, illustrated by Tom Pohrt.

Lopez is the recipient of a Literature Award from the American Academy of Arts and Letters, a Lannan Foundation Award, a Pushcart Prize in fiction, and a PEN Syndicated Fiction Award, and he has been a Guggenheim Fellow.

He contributes regularly to *Harper's*, *The New York Times*, *The North American Review*, *Orion*, *American Short Fiction*, *The Paris Review*, and other publications.

A Note on the Type

This book was set in Bodoni Book, a typeface named after Giambattista Bodoni (1740–1813), the celebrated printer and type designer of Parma. The Bodoni types of today were designed not as faithful reproductions of any one of the Bodoni fonts but rather as a composite, modern version of the Bodoni manner. Bodoni's innovations in type style included a greater degree of contrast in the thick and thin elements of the letters and a sharper and more angular finish of details.

Composed by Crane Typesetting Service, Inc., West Barnstable, Massachusetts
Printed and bound by Arcata Graphics/Fairfield, Fairfield, Pennsylvania
Designed by Anthea Lingeman